Joshua's voice came out flat and strained.

"My sister trusted me, and I let her down. I was all she had."

He let the silence settle upon the cab of his pickup. Emma hadn't moved since he'd started talking.

"That's why you're helping me, isn't it?" she finally said.

"I don't know." Joshua looked down at her. "But it could be."

Emma seemed to consider that. "So, I'm kind of like a sister to you?"

"No," Joshua said firmly without even thinking.

"I see," Emma said, her voice flat. "I'm sure she was special."

Joshua reached over and traced Emma's jawline with his thumb. "You're special, too. That's why you're not like a sister to me."

Emma smiled slightly at that, and Joshua felt his mood lift…

Janet Tronstad grew up on her family's farm in central Montana and now lives in Turlock, California, where she is always at work on her next book. She has written over forty books, many of them set in the fictitious town of Dry Creek, Montana, where the men spend the winters gathered around the potbellied stove in the hardware store and the women make jelly in the fall.

Books by Janet Tronstad

Love Inspired

Dry Creek

Dry Creek Sweethearts
A Dry Creek Courtship
Snowbound in Dry Creek
Small-Town Brides
"A Dry Creek Wedding"
Silent Night in Dry Creek
Wife Wanted in Dry Creek
Small-Town Moms
"A Dry Creek Family"
Easter in Dry Creek
Dry Creek Daddy
His Dry Creek Inheritance
His Dry Creek Legacy

Visit the Author Profile page at Harlequin.com for more titles.

His Dry Creek Legacy

Janet Tronstad

LOVE INSPIRED
INSPIRATIONAL ROMANCE

LOVE INSPIRED®

INSPIRATIONAL ROMANCE

PLEASE RECYCLE
THIS PRODUCT IS RECYCLABLE

Recycling programs
for this product may
not exist in your area.

ISBN-13: 978-1-335-48892-3

His Dry Creek Legacy

This edition published by arrangement with Harlequin Books S.A.

For questions and comments about the quality of this book, please contact us at CustomerService@Harlequin.com.

Love Inspired
22 Adelaide St. West, 40th Floor
Toronto, Ontario M5H 4E3, Canada
www.Harlequin.com

Printed in U.S.A.

It is better to trust in the Lord
than to put confidence in man.
—*Psalms* 118:8

This book is dedicated to my awesome readers.
You have encouraged me over the years
in my writing and I am thankful to you.

Chapter One

Joshua Spencer glanced down at the cigar box lying beside him on the seat of his old ranch pickup. A blizzard raged outside, and the mountain road beneath him was icy, but that box gave him a sense of triumph. His plan would work. With the golden palm tree stamped on the top of its flip-up lid and its belly stuffed with hundred-dollar bills, it would be irresistible to anyone, especially the young and very pregnant Emma Smitt.

Just then his pickup hit a frozen rut and slid to the left. He had to focus on wrestling the front wheels back to the road despite the heavy snow outside that made it hard for him to see. He did it, but a frown started growing on his forehead, and it only deepened when he was back on track and had coaxed his pickup a few yards farther down the road.

"Aw, who am I kidding?" he muttered before slapping the flat of his hand against the steering wheel. She wasn't going to trust him enough to even let him give her the money.

If anyone should know that it was him. At twenty-nine years old, he was a master of distrust. Everyone thought he was completely carefree. He laughed; he joked. He dated as widely as any single man, and the fact that he never seemed to settle on one woman was marked down to his fun-loving ways. But, in the quiet of the night, he knew that what people saw was only the mask he wore. In truth, he stood alone because he never trusted anyone. In Emma's shoes, he wouldn't take that money either. The bills could be counterfeit or, worse, a trap of some kind.

And yet she needed the money. He understood from the attorney that Emma was broke and so close to giving birth that she must be frantic. All of his instincts told him she was by herself in these isolated mountains with no medical person in sight. He knew what facing trouble without help was like.

Joshua pressed down harder on the gas pedal. The storm was almost blinding by now. He might be a fool, but she was a bigger one, and he was determined to save her. He had been worried about Emma ever since he saw her a month ago, hundreds of miles east of here in the small ranching town of Dry Creek, Montana. She had been walking out of the church after Eli Rosen's funeral when it struck him that she was used to being alone. For one thing, she hadn't been exiting the funeral like everyone else with her head bowed humbly over a tear-soaked tissue. Granted, she had not known Eli, the owner of the prosperous Rosen Ranch, but most people would have made some small concession to the grief of others by bowing. Instead, she walked with her back stiff and straight; her head held high like she was the queen of her own parade. It was clear she didn't want anyone to think she was part of what was happening. She didn't want to be approached.

According to snatches of scandalized gossip Joshua had overheard earlier that day, Emma had just found out on the way to the church that Eli's grown son, Junior, had played her false, leaving her unwed and pregnant when he died in a vehicle crash some weeks earlier. Unknown to Emma, Junior had been lying in the Dry Creek cemetery for over a month.

Joshua knew Emma's illegal wedding must be tearing her apart. She had apparently given her heart to Junior. Her vows had been sincere. Of course, Junior's vows had been worthless since he already had a wife that he'd kept secret from Emma. She had a right to her anger. But she hadn't needed to put the walls around her so high that she refused the quiet financial help offered by the church's pastor as he stood at the door of the sanctuary after that funeral.

"I'm fine," she'd announced that day in a voice that was forced and a little too loud. Then she turned, and her blazing eyes challenged any of those standing around to question her. "Just fine."

Joshua saw himself in her at that moment. He was trying to think of some way to persuade her to accept the pastor's help when she stomped out of the church with her shoulders squared and her long chestnut hair bouncing in rhythm with her firm steps.

He turned then and saw many of his neighbors gathered behind him watching the woman. He could tell that they had expected a repentant mouse of a girl and were taken back when they'd gotten a fiery tiger woman instead.

Joshua couldn't help but follow Emma outside that day. He caught up with her when she was almost to the car and reached to open the door for her.

"Leave me alone," she hissed. But her anger seemed subdued, and she was looking down. Waves of her sun-streaked hair fell forward, hiding everything but the tip of her nose.

"I want to help." He wasn't the best one to offer, but no one else had stepped forward.

"I don't want your help," she'd answered, glancing up at him. "And that ranch can fall off the ends of the earth for all I care and take Bailey Rosen with it."

Okay, Joshua thought as he took a step back. She did not know him, but she must have guessed that he worked at the Rosen Ranch. Bailey Rosen was Junior's real wife and as much of a boss as the ranch had now, so he could understand that resentment from Emma. Joshua decided he had no choice but to walk away. But then she turned her face so the others couldn't see the tears that she had been fighting. That meant he alone saw them. Her hazel eyes glistened with pain as she briefly met his gaze.

"I'm sorry I said that about Bailey," she whispered. "She was nice to me in the meeting with the attorney."

Emma looked back down at her fingers pressing against the car handle. She was balanced on a thin edge of pride; she needed to open that door herself or she would burst into sobs—and that would humiliate her further.

He felt his gut twist when those eyes pleaded with him to leave her alone while, at the same time, crying out for help. He knew that teeter-totter of emotions all too well. He, too, felt the need to let down his guard sometimes, but a man could not force himself to trust someone. It had to be freely given. Of course, that meant he knew enough not to acknowledge Em-

ma's troubles unless she gave a signal that she wanted
him to, so he stood immobile while she settled herself
in the car and reached into a pocket to pull out a lacy
white handkerchief with a flash of lilac in the corner.
He thought she would use the delicate square to wipe
her eyes, but she just twisted it in her hand instead and
held it, taking a ragged breath as she stared down at it.

After a moment it was clear she wasn't going to say
anything more so Joshua casually stepped forward and
gently closed the door behind her.

Almost immediately, he walked over to the attorney,
who had brought Emma, and demanded to know if she
had anyone to help her when the baby came.

"That's the question," the man said in a rumbly
voice and looked up at Joshua in consternation. "Not
that I should tell you anything—"

"Yes, you should," Joshua replied forcefully and
then tried to smile. He failed. Finally, he was desperate
enough to add, "I used to have a sister. She died, but—"

Joshua stopped. The attorney didn't need to know
all of the bitter details.

"Humph." The attorney studied Joshua a moment
and apparently saw enough to make him relent. "Well,
I guess none of it is all that privileged, and she could
use a bit of *brotherly* concern." The attorney took another measuring look at Joshua and then proceeded.
"The truth is Emma has no one to help. Her father disappeared decades ago. Her mother's dead. Her stepfather is worthless. She has a brother, but he's too young
to help. She was counting on Junior."

Joshua was familiar enough with that kind of a family to know the missing pieces of the story. "Still, Emma's going to need some help."

The attorney gave a shrug. "She doesn't have any money to get help, either. That's why I had the reading of Eli's will today after the funeral. If the baby is Junior's—and I'm confident it is—she'll inherit a good bit from the ranch if she has a DNA test done on her baby to prove it is his. She could at least hire someone on that expectation and arrange to pay them later. I even gave her the name of a reputable midwife who makes those kinds of arrangements. I didn't expect Emma to refuse to have a DNA test for her baby—'not now, not ever' I think she said."

They were silent for a minute.

"Well, it's clear she believed she was married to Junior," Joshua finally said in her defense. "I'm guessing she sees a DNA test as an insult because that means someone—or maybe everyone—thinks she wasn't faithful to the vows she took."

The attorney snorted. "Even Bailey's baby is going to need a test, and she was married to Junior for a long time." He turned to look at where Emma sat in his car. "It's her choice, I guess. But she's only twenty-one years old, and she may not understand how hard life will be for her. The will states it clear. No test, no money. No second chance."

With that, the man turned and, shoulders slumped, walked to his car. It wasn't until the vehicle was out of sight that Joshua noticed the bit of sparkle on the damp ground beside where Emma had opened the car door. He walked over and picked up the wire earring. The front was an oval-shaped piece of silver with several clear sparkling stones hanging from the top. The jewels appeared to be diamonds, which would make it valuable. It must have fallen when she was shaking her head at him. He'd have to return it, of course.

As it turned out, alerting Emma to the fate of that piece of jewelry wasn't easy. He reported it to his boss Bailey, and she called the attorney and left a message telling him that they had an earring of Emma's at the ranch. Since then Joshua moved that earring into the pocket of a new shirt every morning and then prayed for Emma as he put on his boots. Sometimes, after he'd finished feeding cattle or working with the horses, he'd pray again for her. On the tenth day, he decided to give her his poker winnings that he kept in that cigar box.

Time passed, and Joshua's worries about Emma grew until Bailey told him his worrying made her so fretful that she called the attorney who said he was concerned, too, since he'd just talked to the midwife he'd suggested, and Emma hadn't contacted her. The attorney gave Bailey directions to Emma's trailer which she wrote down and gave to Joshua, suggesting he leave after her daughter's talent show that day.

Joshua brought the cigar box with him to the café and, as soon as the show was over, he put on his heaviest winter coat and was on the road within minutes. And now, here he was, watching his wipers work overtime to keep the snow off of his windshield.

He looked down at the hand-drawn map Bailey had made from the attorney's directions. Pencil scratches indicated that Emma's trailer was the third one off this road on a lane called Sunshine. There would be rusty mailboxes on the road, the man had said, although they were abandoned except for maybe Emma's. There weren't any other trailers up that lane that were occupied in the winter. No cabins, either. Joshua had been told he couldn't miss the cutoff. And before he got to it there would be—ah, there it was.

Joshua eased the steering wheel to the left so he could make the turn into the remote gas station with its one lone pump. The place was just where the map said it would be. Most of the neon letters on the big sign were dark, but Joshua could see *GAS* clearly enough. A dim light came through a few small windows at the front of what appeared to be the station itself.

There were no other vehicles around so Joshua parked right in front. Before leaving the cab, he tucked the cigar box under the seat. The wind nipped fiercely at him when he opened the vehicle door, but all he could do was pull the collar on his sheepskin coat higher and then press his dark brown Stetson down to his ears before hurrying through the blowing snow to the gas station.

He saw a notice taped to the front door that said *Please don't kiss the bird*. He decided it was someone's idea of a joke, although who it was supposed to amuse up here he didn't know.

Warm air and the smell of roasting hot dogs greeted Joshua when he stepped inside the place. Then he heard a raucous screech followed by "Kiss the bird. Kiss the bird. Good boys kiss the bird."

Joshua turned and saw an African Grey parrot in a cage hanging in the far corner. The bird had stopped talking and cocked its head to study him.

"Well, aren't you a pretty bird?" Joshua complimented the parrot. The bird's head was mostly gray with a heart-shaped patch of white that outlined both black eyes. Red tail feathers showed under the dark gray feathers.

The bird nodded at Joshua but didn't answer with another request. Instead it started to peck at something on the bottom of its cage.

Joshua stood on the concrete floor, letting the snow melt off his boots. Who would think a parrot would be here in the middle of nowhere? The station looked like it had been out of business for the past twenty years. He saw an old, stained towel on the floor by the door and figured it was to clean up the puddle the snow left at one's feet. He reached for it and soaked up all of the water around him.

"Coming" a man's voice called from the other side of the closed door that stood behind the counter.

Joshua kept looking around. To his left there was a patchwork of dusty auto parts stacked on a shelf. Oil cans lined the wall. To his right, red-wrapped candy bars, bags of chips, and a rolling hot-dog cooker covered the corner of a large worn counter.

Just then the door behind the counter opened, and a lanky, gray-haired man stepped out of what must be his living quarters. An old tattoo showed through his white T-shirt, and *Max* was embroidered on the cap he wore.

"Can I help you?" the man asked as he stepped up and leaned on the counter. "Coffee's hot. You look like you could use some. It's in the back, but I can get it. Free of charge."

"I don't have time. Max, is it?" Joshua pulled his gloves off so his hands could get warm. "Mostly I just want some directions."

"Yeah, I'm Max."

"Kiss the bird," the parrot demanded again from its corner.

"No one's going to kiss you today, Cupid," Max scolded the parrot and, smiling, turned back to Joshua.

"Cupid?" Joshua couldn't help asking. "That's some name. Where'd you get the bird?"

"A buddy of mine had him," Max said as he walked around the counter and pulled a canvas cover down on the bird's cage. "That'll keep him quiet. My buddy named him Cupid for the Valentine shape those white feathers make on his face. He's the one who taught him to ask for kisses. He thought it was real cute. I've tried to teach him to ask customers to buy more gas, but he doesn't take to it."

Joshua chuckled. "Can't make a storekeeper out of him, huh?"

"I guess not," Max said with a shrug. "Maybe I should have tried teaching him to give directions instead. Although, not too many folks get lost this far into the mountains. They either know where they're going or they don't come. Least not in this kind of weather."

"It is rough out there," Joshua admitted. "I'm looking for Emma on Sunshine Lane, though, and I wanted to get there sooner rather than later."

The man didn't move, but his eyes grew chilly. "She doesn't get much company. Doesn't want it, either— except for Tommy Two, of course."

"She's got someone with her, then?" Joshua felt foolish. His instincts had been wrong; that rarely happened. He was relieved that there was someone with her though. Tommy Two was an odd name, but he might be okay. She probably had a midwife on call and everything. "Is that her boyfriend?"

Joshua knew he had no business adding that last bit. Just because he'd prayed for her every day for several weeks didn't mean that he had any right to be wondering about her romantic life. He supposed he was just curious if she had managed to overcome her distrust enough to be attached to another man after what had happened. Joshua would want that for her if she was his sister.

"How well do you know Emma?" the gray-haired man asked suspiciously.

"Not that well," Joshua admitted. "I've just come up here to check on her. I'm a horse wrangler from the Rosen Ranch down by—"

"I know where it is," Max said as his lips pursed in disapproval. He crossed his bony arms. "And high time that husband of hers sent someone up to see that she's not freezing to death." He shook his head. "A decent husband would do the checking himself. And he would have done it a few months ago by my reckoning. I don't care if he is off doing some fancy rodeo work like she said."

Joshua froze. The facts had all been laid out in the meeting the attorney had with Emma and the other heirs after Eli's funeral. She should have accepted it by now. Junior was dead. He wasn't riding rodeo, at least not anywhere on this earth.

"We'll take good care of Emma at the ranch," Joshua said cautiously, looking Max in the eye. She was the important one here. Bailey had already told him to bring her back if possible.

Max finally nodded and jerked his head toward the road going upward. "You best get going, then. Emma's place is a mile, maybe a mile and a half, up that hill to the left. It's steep, but she'll be there."

"Thanks," Joshua said as he turned to leave.

"Wait a minute," Max said, and when Joshua turned around, he was holding out a small waxed bag with three cooked hot dogs in it. "For Tommy. Tell him they're from me. He'll thank you for them."

Joshua reached for his pocket. "How much do I owe you?"

"No need to pay," the man said. "Tommy Two and I have a deal. I feed him hot dogs, and he chases away the squirrels in the summer."

"Does he have a real job—this Tommy?" Joshua couldn't help but wonder who was going to support Emma's baby when the time came. No man who chased squirrels for a living would be able to do it.

Max smirked. "Ask Tommy Two yourself about his job—but be ready to run when you do."

Joshua took the bag of hot dogs and turned to the door. With the overcast clouds and the continuing snow, darkness was going to come fast up here.

Joshua stepped out of the gas station and back into the blizzard. He had to admit that he wasn't looking forward to meeting this Tommy guy. Joshua had known punk kids who had odd names like that when over a decade ago he had greatly disappointed all of his relatives by being sent away for a stint in Montana's juvenile detention system—just like he'd been sent away earlier from his parents' home when the state intervened after his sister died. Mostly, he'd been shuttled from one uncle's family to another with brief periods in foster homes or other places. And mostly he was sent to whoever needed help on their farm.

A large drift prevented Joshua from getting all of the way to Emma's trailer so he parked his pickup on the side of the rugged lane. Then he took his long wool scarf out of the glove compartment, tied it around his ears, put his Stetson back on and opened the door. He grabbed the bag of hot dogs before facing the swirling snow.

He hadn't walked a yard before flakes gathered on his eyelashes and he could hardly see. He wiped them away so he could study the roof of Emma's trailer. A stove pipe stuck straight up, but he couldn't see any trace of smoke coming out of it. The snow on the roof wasn't even melted around the pipe so the thing hadn't been in use for the past few hours at least. An ancient red pickup stood beside the trailer, though, so she must be there—unless Tommy had his own vehicle and had taken her someplace.

Joshua decided that, if she wasn't there, he would leave a note on her door so that she knew she was welcome to come to the Rosen Ranch if she wanted. He'd find someplace to leave the cigar box with the earring inside on top of the money and tell her all about it in the note, too. One of the napkins Max had put in the bag with the hot dogs would do for his message.

He was several yards from the trailer when he heard a low growl. The sound was so soft that he thought it was the wind at first. Then he saw the dog rise up from a snow drift and bare its teeth.

"Nice doggie," Joshua muttered with a cautious smile. The canine almost looked like an arctic wolf. It was covered with snow but didn't try to shake the flakes off like a dog normally would—probably because the beast was intensely focused on Joshua and didn't want to relax its gaze. The animal barked, but not in a friendly manner.

Then Joshua remembered what he had in his hands.

He pulled out a hot dog and threw it to the canine. "Tommy won't miss one of these."

The dog kept looking at him, but it didn't seem as set on attacking. The animal didn't move from the white drift, though, and that's when Joshua saw a small black boot sticking out from the snow.

He made quick work of the several yards between him and the boot and, soon, was kneeling down on the other side of the drift looking at the pale face of Emma Smitt. Her eyes were closed. His heart clenched in fear. He wondered how long she had been out here. He saw where the dog had been curled up beside her, but the canine wasn't big enough to keep her from freezing for long. Emma's chestnut hair was mostly pulled back under a black knitted cap, but some strands were pressed to her head. Except for where the dog had been, she was almost buried in the snow. Joshua brushed the white off her forehead, and she slowly opened her eyes. For the first time, he saw that their natural hazel color was streaked with gold. They were the prettiest sight he had ever seen.

"You okay?" Joshua asked as he started sweeping the snow away as fast as he could. Now was not the time to be thinking about how beautiful her eyes were.

"I fell," she whispered and held up a small crumpled envelope. "I got the mail. Twisted my ankle, I think."

Joshua turned to look and saw where she'd crawled for some distance, dragging her foot. He was right that she had some grit to her, he thought.

"You shouldn't be out here alone," he said as he carefully felt her arms for any broken bones. He purposely avoided her belly; he hadn't ever touched a pregnant woman there, and he wasn't going to start today.

He didn't want to make her uncomfortable. "Where's Tommy?"

Emma smiled. "Tommy Two? He's with me."

Joshua squinted and looked around. The storm had cleared some. "I don't see him."

He wondered if Emma was having delusions from a concussion. She looked vaguely confused and might have hit her head. "Where does it hurt?"

"Nowhere," she whispered, but her eyes were still not focused.

"Where did Tommy go?" Joshua could use some help if he had to carry Emma back inside in this snow. She wasn't heavy, but he knew she'd probably rather have this other man lift her. She didn't seem to be thinking clearly. The fact that she didn't hurt likely meant she was almost frozen.

"He'll be back on duty when he's finished the hot dog," Emma added softly.

"You mean—" Joshua twirled around to stare at the animal, who had growled so fiercely at him, swallow the last bit of the meat.

"That's Tommy?" Joshua raised his voice. He couldn't believe it. "You've been out here with nobody but a dog to help you?" Even a squirrel-chasing deadbeat would be better than that.

"His name is Tommy Two," she replied and tried to sit up. "And I see Max every few days—well, at least once a week." She looked at Joshua and smiled like he was some knight in white armor. "And now you're here."

She actually sighed.

Joshua frowned. He was only here because he had that earring. And he wanted to give her his poker money. But he might not have come. She had no right to rely on such a flimsy rescue plan. He didn't like people trusting him like that. Still, that smile of hers was sweet.

Then her smile wavered, and her eyelids slowly started to lower.

Emma let her eyes flutter until they closed. It would just be for a minute, she promised herself. Now that the nice man with those nice eyes was here she could... She felt herself drifting off and could not stop it. Everything was fuzzy. She'd been tense for so long, and she finally felt peaceful.

"Emma." The voice above her was insistent. "Emma."

"I'm okay," she muttered as she tried to turn. A mountain of white seemed to surround her. She vaguely remembered she had fallen and hurt herself. There had been pain. But it was all gone now. She felt like she was rolling around in some cozy snow globe.

"We have to move you," the voice continued. "Work with me. My pickup is close. When you get in, I'll drive you back to the gas station. It's warm there. I doubt your trailer has any heat left."

"Out of wood," she admitted. She had been going to get more, and then the storm came. She should have done better. And something else should trouble her.

A strong pair of arms reached around her, gently pulling her up.

Emma felt her eyes partially open. "I'm sorry I—" Then she remembered and blinked; her eyes opened wide in panic. "My baby! I need to protect my baby from the fall." That's why she'd twisted when she went down.

Just then she felt a tiny reassuring kick against the side of her stomach. She placed her hand where the kick had been.

"Thank you, sweet baby," she murmured.

It was silent for a minute. The man was looking at her strangely. She wondered if he thought she was speaking that endearment to him. She couldn't summon up the energy to tell him she wasn't.

"We need to get you out of the cold," the man above her finally said. His voice was a pleasing baritone. The sound was faintly familiar, but the only man she'd talked to lately had been Max. That was not his voice. She squinted into the shadows and tried to see the face beneath that Stetson. She could only see his chin and the side of his cheek, but she knew. It was the man from the funeral—the one who insisted on walking her to the car.

"Why are you here?" she demanded, trying to put some muscle into her words. Men only respected strength. She never let her guard down around them. Her tone wasn't stern enough so she tried to glare at him with her eyes. He didn't look afraid.

"Remember me? Joshua," he said. "I came to help you." Then he smiled and caught her hand before it fell back. He took off his gloves and slipped one of them onto the hand. "That'll keep you warmer." He reached out for her other hand and, when she lifted it, put the other glove on it. "Stay with me. We need to get you in the pickup so your baby will not be cold."

"He gave me a kick," she said softly. She knew she should refuse to talk to the man, but he didn't seem to scare away, and she was tired. The gloves still held his body heat and her fingers were starting to tingle. She was warming up.

He nodded. She watched the flakes of snow fall off his hat as he moved.

"We can't stay here," he continued. "When I count to three, let's both make an effort to get you up."

Emma wasn't ready on the count, but she did the best she could and found herself standing upright. Joshua had his arm around her to steady her. Tommy Two was racing around her, but not barking. Within three long steps, Emma was waking up, and she started to shiver.

Joshua opened the passenger side door for her and almost lifted her onto the high seat. Tommy Two jumped up and curled himself around her feet. When Joshua closed the door, Emma felt the temperature rise because there was no wind inside.

She was glad that Joshua managed to drive down the lane to Max's place quickly. When they got there, he had to step out of the pickup and pound on the gas-station door because Max had locked up for the evening. Emma was beginning to realize she could have died out there in the snow. She would not have been able to crawl to the station, and she would not have made it up the road to her trailer. She had intended to walk down to Max's place after she got the mail. She was out of almost everything and planned to see if Max had some milk and eggs he could sell her. She had thought he might have some spare wood, too.

She was glad when Joshua came back with a wool blanket in his arms. He wrapped the blanket around her and helped her make the steps to the gas-station store. Tommy Two walked along beside them. Max was watching and opened the door when they arrived.

The blast of warm air made Emma gasp hard. Her whole body tingled.

She felt Joshua stop, and Max turned to stare at her.

"Is it the baby?" Max asked as his eyes went wide. "That sounded like a pain coming."

"Kiss the baby," the parrot heralded from her cage in the corner.

"I want to kiss my baby," Emma answered the bird back.

She saw Joshua look at her, his eyes filled with worry.

"Don't worry," Emma said then with a grin. "My baby's not coming yet. My fingers and toes are just starting to feel those sharp spikey things like they do when they warm up. It feels funny."

"You'd tell us, though," Joshua said. "If it was your time. You'd let us know?"

"Of course," Emma said. "But I have weeks yet."

She thought a moment and added, "Well, at least a week. Almost. A few days, anyway."

Joshua gasped at that.

"Lord, be with us," he muttered aloud. "You should have a plan in place already. You know the baby is coming. You're going to be a mother."

"Kiss the mother," the parrot suggested, sounding insistent.

Emma loved thinking about being a mother.

"Kiss the mother," the bird demanded even louder.

"You better do it," Max intoned grimly, talking to Joshua. "Once Cupid gets an idea in that head of his, he's determined to make it happen. We'll be here all night."

"It's okay," Emma said with a wave to Cupid. "I don't need a kiss."

"Kiss the—" Cupid started to screech.

"Oh," Joshua said as he turned, bent down, and went to kiss her. Emma figured he'd been aiming for her cheek, but she'd moved when she saw him coming, and they had collided. She'd meant to avoid the kiss altogether. Instead, their lips had met squarely.

"Kiss," Cupid cooed at the barely audible smack on Emma's lips.

Well, Emma thought, that had been…unusual, she decided. There had been no lightning flash or swooning, but his lips did have a lingering tenderness that was nice. If it had been longer—or even intentional—maybe it would have been more stirring.

Not that she needed that kind of excitement, Emma told herself as she stepped away. The kiss did remind her, though, that before the bird interfered, this man had uttered a prayer like it was as natural as breathing. She'd seen him inside and outside the church that day. "Are you a minister?"

"Me?" Joshua sounded surprised. "No. I've started to attend church again, but I'm a horse wrangler on the Rosen Ranch."

"Oh." Emma frowned. One thing was certain in her life right now—she wasn't going to rely on any man again. She had learned her lesson with Junior. She didn't know why she was even considering unbending a little with this man. If he had been a minister, that might explain it. Maybe it was because he rescued her today.

"Well," Max said with a twinkle in his eyes as he started to lead Emma farther into his store, "I'm not sure it's a compliment to a man for a woman to think he kisses like a, uh, minister."

"A minister is not a monk," Joshua snapped back. He went to the other side of her and started holding her other elbow. Emma thought he looked agitated.

"The kiss was fine," she protested.

Max chuckled as he glanced over at Joshua. "I'm sure Cupid will have you doing better before you know it."

"That bird needs to mind his own business," Joshua said.

Emma was between the two men, and they were holding her up as they kept walking. She felt them each tug her in their direction.

"Cupid is minding his business," Max said as he kept walking. "Matchmaking is a hobby of his."

"Strange hobby if you ask me," Joshua said.

Emma reached down as best she could and brushed her hand against Tommy Two's back. His fur was cold and wet, but he steadied her. The dog she trusted. At least she didn't have to worry about him taking sides in a battle over what a bird should be doing.

Emma let the two men help her to the bed in the back room.

"Just lie down, and I'll get some more blankets for you," Max said as he helped her sit down on the bed. Then he pulled off her boots and fussed over her.

Joshua stood some feet away, looking at her with a puzzled expression on his face. She didn't have time to worry about him right now. He might have pretty eyes, but—now that he was not a minister out to help people—she wasn't quite sure why he was here. Nice guys didn't just drop out of the sky; she knew that better than most. They certainly didn't kiss strange women when they did so.

"Why do you care?" she murmured.

"I had a sister," he said softly.

"And I remind you." That was a nice reason, Emma thought as she gripped the envelope she'd carried in with her and closed her eyes. It was so nice and warm inside this place. She hadn't felt this relaxed for such a long time.

"Night, night baby," she whispered as she put her hand on her stomach before readying herself for sleep.

She thought she heard the man whisper *Night, night* too.

She smiled as she let the darkness fall. The envelope was from her young brother, but she'd have to open it in the morning. She hoped he wasn't in trouble. Then she remembered he usually was.

Chapter Two

Joshua woke with a jolt of pain in his back and the feel of something heavy on his feet. A thin light was coming in through the high windows of the gas station. He lifted himself up on an elbow and looked down, only to realize that the weight at his feet was nothing more than that dog. Tommy Two had pulled on the blankets Joshua had used last night, hauling him off the air mattress as he did so. Joshua had landed on the hard concrete floor, and the dog had sat on him. Joshua noted that the beast looked smug and not a bit repentant about the whole situation.

"You think you're pretty smart, don't you?" Joshua whispered to the dog. The animal gave a half-hearted growl in response, but he didn't give up his grip on the blankets. He did finally roll off Joshua's feet, though.

"Thanks for that much," Joshua said as he rubbed his head. He had to get up, anyway. He stretched his legs and yawned before standing. He noticed the bird's cage was still covered, and Cupid was quiet.

"So far, so good," Joshua murmured to himself. He didn't much care for that matchmaking bird.

Joshua had slept with his socks on, but he looked around for his boots. They were near the far wall. The dog had moved them and likely chewed on them while he was doing so. Joshua hobbled over to the wall. He heard a muffled conversation from the other room and stood still. He could not make out the words.

Joshua leaned against the wall and pushed his feet down into his boots. The tones sounded pleasant, and then the voices spiked.

"He was already *married*?" Max yelled indignantly. His voice carried through the door and into the store. It might have even made it down the mountain and into Missoula. "What kind of a no-good scoundrel was he?"

Emma spoke too softly for Joshua to make out her words, but he figured she was agreeing with Max. Joshua didn't want to disturb them so he walked back over to the air mattress and kneeled down to roll it up. He let the air out slowly. It made him feel good that someone was outraged on Emma's behalf. Most of the people in Dry Creek would have given Junior a good scolding if he hadn't died before they had known anything about what he'd done.

Joshua finished rolling up the air mattress, and he found the cord to tie it in place. Then he turned to the blankets. Tommy Two growled and put his paws on the blankets so Joshua decided to leave them alone for now. By that time, the smell of frying bacon floated through the air.

Joshua's stomach grumbled. He wouldn't mind a fine breakfast. Maybe there were eggs, too. And coffee. He did like a good fried egg with his bacon.

A metal lid slammed against a counter in the back. At least that's what it sounded like to Joshua. It must have shaken the windows in that room. He feared for the eggs if they weren't already in the pan. He supposed they could be scrambled, if necessary.

"What kind of a will is that?" Max's voice demanded loudly enough for Joshua to hear.

Joshua knew then that Emma was getting to the heart of the matter. Eli Rosen had been desperate to leave a blood heir behind him after Junior died. Eli had willed half of his ranch to Bailey Rosen, Junior's legal wife, if the child she bore proved to be Junior's child and kept the Rosen name. That meant Emma, according to that will, had a chance to claim half of the Rosen Ranch for herself and her baby as long as the child was proven to be Junior's and would go by the Rosen name. If Emma didn't do the tests by the set deadline, she and her child would receive nothing, and it would all go to Bailey and her family.

Suddenly, Max stepped out of his quarters, a large metal spatula in his hand which he shook at Joshua. "What are you doing up here? Spying on Emma?"

Joshua looked at the older man and felt his smile slide off his face. "I came up because I'm—we're—worried about Emma and thought she'd do better at the Rosen Ranch. We can give her—"

Max snorted in disbelief. "Don't tell me this is charity for you folks. You're more likely to murder her in her sleep than do anything helpful for her."

"What are you talking about?" Joshua said and scowled.

"You and that will." Max brandished the spatula around like it was a medieval weapon of some sort. He stopped it finally. "Your boss would do better if something happened to Emma and her baby. Your boss would have the whole ranch, then. How does Emma know you're not planning some accident? Are you saying she should trust you because you're just naturally good folks? Pure as the driven snow your whole life long?"

Joshua saw no need to inform the other man that he had not been pure most of his life. It had only been a few months ago that he'd gone before the church and given up gambling. Until that time, he'd never exactly cheated at poker, but he'd used his bantering to distract other players so he managed to win—a lot. He was known for his golden tongue.

"I'm not always the best in my talking," Joshua found himself admitting without thinking, and he winced. Why would he confess that to a man he barely knew?

"So you use a few bad words," Max said contemptuously. "No one said you were a choirboy."

That was the problem, Joshua thought. He could sound like a choirboy if he wanted. Somehow, though, his conscience had turned on him that day in church. He meant to give up the gambling, but not his golden tongue—he needed that. He used to be able to charm a man's last dollar from his pocket. Last Sunday he couldn't even pass around the offering plate without wanting to give it all back. His easy-talking days were over, and he was in trouble.

"Is it such a crime to want to help someone?" Joshua finally asked, wishing he could explain it better.

Max grunted. "Nobody goes to the kind of trouble you did yesterday unless there's something in it for them. You must have wanted to get here really bad to drive all this way in that kind of a storm."

All of his life Joshua had relied on his glib talk to rescue him from awkward spots like this, and now he had nothing.

"Maybe I wanted redemption," Joshua whispered, doing the best he could to explain. Not that helping Emma would make up for not helping his sister.

"What's that got to do with Emma?" Max asked indignantly. "She doesn't want charity, you know."

"I figured that," Joshua said.

Max was still glaring at him. "Why do you think I live way out here? I don't trust people at all. And Emma doesn't, either."

"Look," Joshua said, "if you're so worried, why don't you come to the ranch with her and see for yourself."

The man seemed speechless at that offer.

Then Joshua heard the light brush of a footstep and turned to the doorway that separated the store from Max's quarters. There stood Emma with a blanket wrapped around her shoulders and her hair pulled back with a plain rubber band. Her eyes were big, and her face was as white as the piece of paper she held up. She leaned against the doorjamb.

"I need to go into Missoula," she said to Max. "The letter is from Tommy."

"How is the boy?" the older man asked as he turned from Joshua and focused on Emma. He seemed to forget the spatula as it hung at his side. "Your stepfather taking good care of him?"

Joshua could smell the bacon starting to burn, but he didn't say anything. He could tell from the tension between the two that something was up.

"I don't know," Emma said; her voice was toneless. "He—my brother—it's hard to know."

"What's the letter say?" Max demanded to know.

Emma turned the paper so that a crayon drawing of a stick figure curled up into a ball showed. "It says *Me Gone*."

"What does that mean?" Max asked in a puzzled voice.

"I don't know," Emma said. "But I need to go see him. He's afraid."

By this time even Joshua had forgotten about the bacon. A young child was in trouble. "How can I help?"

Emma and Max both looked at him in surprise as though they had forgotten he was even there.

"The boy—" Max started and spread his hands as though he was at a loss for words. "He's a good kid. Doesn't deserve the hand he's been dealt in life."

"I need to go to him," Emma repeated, this time speaking to Joshua. "He's only seven years old. My pickup doesn't work. Can you—" Emma stopped as though she had just remembered her pride and her earlier suspicions of him. She swallowed. "I'm sorry for how I acted that day at the funeral."

"I'm happy to drive you," Joshua said quickly. "And forget about the other. You were under a lot of stress."

Emma blushed. "Thank you."

Max glanced between Joshua and Emma and seemed to reach some conclusion. "I'll follow in my pickup," he said with a look at Joshua. "But I need to put in a new battery before I can go so I'll be a few minutes. And I need time to get Cupid's food ready. And the cage."

"The bird will ride with you?" Joshua asked.

"Of course," Max said.

"Okay, then," Joshua said.

Max stepped back into his quarters.

"I need to get Tommy Two's dog food, too," Emma said as she took a step and then winced. "I forgot about my foot."

"I can go up and get what you need," Joshua offered.

Emma looked down at herself. "I better go, too. My ankle isn't so bad this morning. Besides, I need to change my clothes. And get my suitcase that I packed for—"

Joshua nodded in relief. She had remembered. "For the hospital," he added. "I suppose you have some baby clothes and a nightgown for yourself."

"That's not what I have," Emma said softly. "I packed all my pictures in case I needed to leave the trailer. Did it back in the fire season. That's all I have there that's important."

"Oh," Joshua said. Maybe the hospital had baby clothes. He knew they had those gowns. It could be women didn't even need to pack a suitcase anymore. He was sure they still needed money, though, so he was glad that cigar box was still tucked under the seat in his pickup. "Well, I'll drive you up to your place when you're ready."

Emma turned and hobbled into the back room.

Joshua went to the washroom off the business part of the building and got his hair combed and his teeth brushed. He straightened his clothes. It had only taken him a few minutes, but when he stepped back into the store, Emma stood there ready to go, and Max held out a toasted bacon sandwich to each of them.

"The eggs broke on the floor," Max said as Joshua took his sandwich. "Sorry. It was the last of them."

"No problem," Joshua said. "This will do me. Thank you."

The bacon was almost burned, and the toast was barely warm, but all together it tasted good to Joshua.

"Yum," Emma added once she'd finished her sandwich.

Max looked pleased. "I don't often have company in to eat. Well, except for Tommy Two."

Joshua looked over and saw the dog was enjoying his own breakfast beside the counter. None of it was burned.

Joshua turned from the dog back to Emma. "Is there some reason you named your dog after your brother?"

She ducked her head and started toward the door. "It's Tommy's dog. He likes things that he cares about to match. His real mother is Mommy and I'm Mommy Two."

"Oh," Joshua said. He'd known a lot of children in his life, and none of them had ever come up with a system like that.

Emma limped toward the door. Then she stopped right in front of it.

"Here," Joshua said as he went over to her and offered her an arm to hold onto. Of course she couldn't make it along that icy path alone.

"Thank you," Emma said stiffly as she took his arm.

"I'll be ready to go when you get back from the trailer," Max said as he walked toward his back room. "You two be careful, now."

The older man went into his living space.

Joshua decided he didn't know anything about the

moods that overtook pregnant women. For the first time, it occurred to him that he was in over his head. He'd done fine with the blizzard and could do that again any day, but figuring out Emma was beyond him.

He felt his shirt pocket for that earring and assured himself it was still there. He wondered when would be the best time to give it to Emma. Not now, he decided.

The store door stuck slightly, and Joshua had to push it. The snow was no longer falling when they stepped through. Instead, the flakes pleasantly gleamed in the sunlight as they lay on the ground. The snow also draped the tall pines around the gas station. It was pretty, Joshua decided, as he led Emma to his pickup. Maybe all of that natural beauty would make her feel calmer.

Emma tucked herself into the pickup. The upholstery on the seat was cold. She missed having Tommy Two at her feet, but the dog would be happier at Max's place than going with her up to the trailer. She'd let the dog ride on her feet later.

When Joshua got inside the cab, he turned the engine on and moved a dial on the dashboard. "It takes a while to warm up."

"That's okay," Emma said. "The heater doesn't even work on my pickup. Of course, the brakes are shot, too, so…" She left the sentence unfinished. She was living hand to mouth and, as often as not, the hand didn't have much in it. Without Max's help, she would be hungry some, maybe most, days. She didn't want Joshua to know how things were with her, though. "I can give you gas money for taking me into Missoula."

She did have those checks still coming from Junior's

account regularly. They were small—three hundred and fifty dollars each month—but they came. That's why she hadn't believed he was dead at first. Junior had set those checks up when they were first married.

"It's not a problem," Joshua said as he started to back up. "It's on the way to the ranch, anyway."

Emma frowned. "But you have to bring me back. That means extra miles."

"You're not coming to the ranch?" Joshua asked as he turned to look at her. He sounded astonished. Emma wondered if she'd said she would go with him and didn't remember. No, she was sure she hadn't.

"I don't think that would be proper," Emma said quietly. "I mean, I appreciate you coming all this way to check on me, but I don't think… No, it wouldn't be comfortable."

By this time, Joshua was facing ahead and driving onto the lane that led up the mountain to her trailer.

"So who's going to drive you to the hospital when you have the baby?" he demanded fiercely.

"I…uh," Emma hesitated. He didn't need to sound so irritated. She had a plan; she just hadn't made sure it would work. "I plan to ask Max."

"He doesn't even have a working battery in his pickup," Joshua said, his voice rising in disbelief. "You would be stuck if you needed to go today."

"Well, he's putting a new one in right now," Emma said, defending her friend. "And I'm going to Missoula today so it's not the day for the baby."

Joshua grunted, but he didn't say anything.

They were both silent for a moment, but just when she thought they had settled everything, Joshua started again and asked, "Is that what your doctor told you?

That the baby wouldn't come when you had other plans?"

"Not every woman needs a doctor," she said, hoping she had enough ice in her voice to stop his nosy questions.

He slowed the pickup to a stop and turned to her. "I can't believe it. You haven't been to a doctor, have you?"

He no longer sounded critical, but it was worse. She knew she'd disappointed him, although why she should care, she didn't know.

"Well, I haven't needed a doctor yet," Emma said in what she thought was a very reasonable tone of voice. "When I do, I'll find one."

"But what about all of the vitamins they want you to take?" Joshua asked. He was still a little agitated. "And the lessons on breathing. My second cousin went on and on about how to breathe with the pains until it sounded like she'd invented the system."

"I can breathe," Emma said. "I've done it my whole life so far and I've survived."

"But you don't have a plan," Joshua lamented as though that were some kind of a crime.

"I do, too, have a plan," she assured him. "When it's time, I'll go down and ask Max to take me to the emergency room in Missoula."

"Yesterday you fell before you even made it down to his place."

"Well, I won't fall when it's important," Emma said emphatically.

He snorted in response, but he did press on the gas again, and they continued the drive up the lane.

Joshua had a scowl on his face, and Emma had to

stop herself from scooting closer to the door. She was amazed she'd ever thought he might be a minister. She didn't know much about church life, but she didn't think a man of the cloth would be as judgmental as this one. They were supposed to be kind.

Joshua had to park his pickup a few yards from the door to her trailer, but she refused to apologize for the inconvenience. The snow drifts were packed solid at the top of her drive.

He just sat there and looked around him at the trees and the trailer.

"I'm sorry you have to park so far away," Emma finally gave in and admitted. "I haven't been able to clear the drive for weeks."

"I should hope you wouldn't be out shoveling snow in your condition," Joshua said.

She didn't answer.

"How'd you even end up here, anyway?" Joshua asked as he opened the driver's side door. He turned back to look at her. "It's beautiful, but you're so far from everything. You're kind of buried out here in the winter."

Emma searched his eyes for any criticism and found none.

"I'm sure it's even more beautiful in the summer," Joshua added thoughtfully. "And peaceful."

"Junior bought the trailer for us," Emma answered, smiling as she remembered. "We were going to live here together. He liked to hunt and fish. And, well, I was going to raise a bunch of Alpine goats. Maybe make some cheese to sell."

Joshua nodded but didn't say anything more as he stepped out of his pickup.

"There are a lot of places where you could raise goats," Joshua said later as he helped Emma out of the passenger side. She felt awkward being so large in her stomach, but he didn't say anything.

"I know there are other places that have them," Emma agreed as they began the slow trek to her front door. But she could do them here and be independent. "I want a job I can do on my own."

She had muttered those last words, and he didn't respond. He may not have even heard her. She hadn't noticed how much work the trailer needed until she looked up as they were walking. There was a thin line of rust around the window by the front door, and the side of the trailer had dents from when that tree had fallen some months ago. She'd meant to change the Army green of the siding, too, but she hadn't had the time or the money.

At least the front steps were solid, Emma thought as they climbed all six of them. Junior had built those stairs the last time he was with her in the trailer.

"The key is under that square pot," Emma said as they stood on the porch.

Joshua bent down and got the key before she remembered. "Oh, I'm sorry. I didn't lock the door yesterday when I went to get the mail."

Joshua nodded as he put the key back under the pot. "I wouldn't have, either."

Emma pushed the door open and stepped inside. She could hear Joshua following her. She could also smell the damp inside the trailer. This time of year, she needed to keep a fire going constantly in the cast-iron woodstove that stood between the living room and the kitchen. There was not much insulation in the walls.

If she didn't keep the fire up, the temperature would fall to freezing inside.

"I'll go get the dog food," Emma said as she turned to the back bedroom.

"I'll come carry it for you," Joshua offered. "You shouldn't be lifting heavy things like that."

Emma hated for him to walk through the trailer. When Junior bought the place, it had been summer and everything looked charming. Now, without the sun, it looked worn-out and depressing.

She pointed to where the bag of dog food was, and Joshua lifted it to his shoulder. The bag was half-empty, and it was the last of the dozen bags that Junior had bought when they moved into the place last year. If it wasn't for the hot dogs that Max kept on his grill, Tommy Two would have already run out of food.

"Why don't you sit a bit while I take this out to the pickup?" Joshua suggested as they walked back into the living room.

"I'll go into my room and change instead." Emma took small steps in that direction.

"Okay. Take it easy," Joshua said as he walked out of the trailer.

She noticed that the temperature didn't even drop when he opened the door. That meant there was no heat left inside her trailer. He probably added that as another check on his list of her faults. No insulation. She was doing the best she could, but he didn't seem to recognize that. Not even he could say the place wasn't clean, but she had to admit to wishing she had fixed the flap of linoleum that had come loose in the kitchen area. After all, this would be her baby's home soon.

Emma went into her room and put on a very large

pink sweatshirt and her one pair of denim maternity jeans. A glance in the mirror told her she needed to comb her hair so she pulled out the rubber band keeping her tresses in a ponytail and brushed her hair vigorously for a couple of minutes.

Then she opened a drawer in the dresser and pulled out her grandmother's handkerchief. The woman had embroidered lilacs in one corner of the white square and used it all her life before passing it down to Emma's own sweet mother. That and the tears the cloth contained was all Emma had inherited from either of them.

She slipped the handkerchief into her jeans pocket and went back into the living room. By that time, Joshua was stomping his boots on the porch to clear off the snow that must have caked onto his soles as he walked back and forth to the pickup.

"Does this go with you?" Joshua pointed at the big brown suitcase on the sofa and walked to it before she could even get there. She was remembering she hadn't latched it.

"It's not closed," Emma said at the same time as Joshua began to lift it. By the time the suitcase started to tilt, Emma was there to guide it back to the sofa. Still, a flurry of white papers flew out of the case and floated to the floor.

"I'm sorry," Joshua said as he let the whole weight of the suitcase rest on the sofa. "I should have checked."

He started to bend down toward the papers that had fallen, but Emma shooed him away.

"I can get these," she said as she scrambled to hide the pages from his view. Finally, she got them all slipped back inside, and she sat down on the sofa beside her things. She was safe.

"You missed this," Joshua said as he pulled out one of the papers that had slid under the sofa.

She noticed Joshua gave her the paper without turning it over. He must be respecting her privacy.

"Thank you," she said, suspiciously. That didn't seem like him.

He nodded in acknowledgment.

She waited for him to ask what she had guarded so closely, but he didn't. Finally, she couldn't stand the silence. "They are drawings Tommy made."

"He must be a very special brother," Joshua said just like they hadn't discussed him earlier.

"He is," Emma agreed. And then thinking that wasn't enough of an explanation if she was going to be gracious, she continued. "He likes to have the drawings with him when he's upset. I'm just keeping them for him."

Joshua didn't say any more as she finished putting all of the drawings inside. Then he again offered to carry the suitcase out to the pickup.

"Please do," she said and then watched him leave with all of her treasures.

She was relieved that Joshua had shown he could be tactful if he put his mind to it. She wondered if she should ask him to remember his manners when he met Tommy. Of course, sometimes that made the meeting worse.

It was her problem anyway. She always got a nervous stomach when she introduced people to her young brother. She never knew what to say. She didn't like to announce that Tommy had Down syndrome like that was the most important thing about him. He was so much more. He could watch baseball on television for hours, although sometimes she suspected he liked the numbers on the uniforms more than anything about the game. He was kind and animals loved him. Above all, though, he was her brother, and they loved each other.

Before she could even get her thoughts all settled, Joshua was back to help her to the pickup. She had a hard climb back into the cab and was grateful for Joshua's silent support.

"Will the suitcase be all right in the back?" he asked before shutting the passenger side door. "I put a tarp over it and the dog food so nothing will get wet. I just didn't think it was a good idea to have Tommy Two and his food both inside with us."

Emma smiled. "It would drive him wild, and we'd have no peace. He's always hungry."

"That's what I figured." Joshua grinned back.

Maybe they would do okay together for the drive down to Missoula, Emma thought optimistically. It seemed like that once Joshua had stated an opinion he didn't keep bringing it back up.

"Maybe we should stop in Missoula, and you could see a doctor," Joshua said as he started the pickup. "I'm happy to pay the bill."

He looked into the rearview mirror and put the pickup into Reverse.

"I take care of my own bills," Emma said slowly, revising every comforting thing she'd just thought about him. The man didn't seem to know how to mind his own business. Of course, how could he know her family's history?

"My grandmother," Emma said softly, "was so poor

she was forced to take charity most of her life. She died ashamed of that. Even my mother, after she married my stepfather, was reduced to being dependent on the pity of others. My stepfather figured there was no reason for him to buy food when my mother could get it as charity if she'd beg for it. He was proud of his cleverness. My mother was broken. She couldn't even get a job. She tried working a couple of times, and he'd do something to get her fired."

"I'm sorry," Joshua said. "That must have been difficult."

"I promised my mother I would do better," Emma said as she reached into her jeans pocket and pulled out the handkerchief. "My grandmother cried into this, and so did my mother. I don't plan to add to those tears."

Only then did Emma realize Joshua had stopped the pickup. He was listening to her intently. "You'll do better. I know you will."

"Thank you," Emma said. "My stepfather caused a lot of my mother's tears."

"I expect he did." Joshua nodded solemnly and then slowly started the pickup forward again.

Emma had no fondness for her stepfather, but she did hope he would be sober and home when they got there. She glanced over at Joshua. She was glad he'd be with her to face the man.

"Is your stepfather violent?" Joshua asked calmly.

Emma froze. "What makes you ask that?"

"I guess we'll see," Joshua murmured when she didn't answer.

Emma was suddenly very nervous. What would she do if her stepfather did have one of his…spells? That's what they all called them, like they were an illness that came upon him for no reason. She wouldn't want Joshua to see that.

Chapter Three

Joshua was relieved that Max was ready to leave when they got back to the gas station. He'd been touched by Emma's story and didn't want to prolong the trip to see her stepfather. While Joshua and Emma waited, the older man flipped the sign in his window from *Open* to *Closed* and left the building carrying the bird cage and whistling for the dog to follow. Max locked the door before turning to examine his business thoughtfully.

"Folks can still get gas at the pump if they have a credit card," Max said in an aside to Joshua as they started walking toward the two pickups. The dog ran to Emma. "I wouldn't want anyone to run out of gas up here."

Joshua could tell that this gas station was important to Max.

"Not many people come by this time of year, anyway." Max glanced at Joshua. "I haven't had a stop in a week—except for you."

Joshua had wondered how the man made a living and wished he'd thought to buy some gas from him.

Suddenly, he had an idea. "I'll give you some money to fill the tank on Emma's pickup when you get back."

"No, you won't," Emma said with a fierce look at Joshua. "I pay for my own."

They walked a few steps in silence, then Max spoke. "My father built this business back in the fifties. I hardly ever leave. I get my social security checks, and I don't need much more."

Joshua nodded. Now that he'd taken a good look at everything, he could easily understand why someone would like to live here. The colors were more intense than on the flatland. The sky was bluer; the snow whiter. The air even smelled extra sweet from all of the pine trees.

When they reached the pickups, they split, and Max headed to his vehicle with his bird.

Joshua noticed that Emma hesitated when the other man left them, but she had a firm grip on Joshua's arm, and it felt natural for them to just continue to his truck.

"I'm glad you decided to come with me," Joshua said as he opened the passenger door with a flourish and helped Emma inside.

"Well, I don't want to ride with that bird," she said and grinned. "Or be forced to kiss it or anyone else, either."

"Hey, I wasn't forced to kiss you," Joshua protested. He felt a little heat on his face. "It's just—a man doesn't like to take kissing directions from a bird."

Emma laughed, and Joshua chuckled along with her. He liked seeing her exhibit a little attitude. It meant she was feeling good.

The dog jumped up to sit on the floorboard at Emma's feet, and then Joshua closed the door. Then he went around and climbed in on the driver's side.

"There's ice under the snow," Emma noted as he started the engine and began the drive down the mountain. "It'll be slippery."

She was right and did not interrupt his concentration as he slowly made his way down to the highway. All along, he kept an eye out to see that Max wasn't having any trouble behind him. The wrong pressure on the gas or the brakes could make a pickup slide off the road and into a slight crevice. He wasn't sure the old man would be able to dig himself out.

When Joshua reached the plowed highway, he started breathing easier.

"I expect it will be hard on you seeing your stepfather." He'd seen the look on Emma's face when he had asked if her stepfather was ever violent. His own father had gotten overly exuberant and fallen down when he was drunk. Joshua never figured that was any better than being violent since it hid the problem longer.

"I'm doing it for Tommy," she said finally.

Joshua glanced over to her. "Do you know the way to his place?"

She nodded. "He never stays all that long anywhere, but he's liked this house that he's renting now. He's been there more than a year. I'm hoping he will stay. And then there's Sherry."

"Sherry?" Joshua asked.

"His new wife," Emma answered. "The fourth."

"Ah," Joshua said.

"I don't know the name of the first woman," Emma continued. "But then there was my mother. Then Tommy's mother. And now Sherry. At least she doesn't come with any children."

"What?" Joshua asked as he looked over. "That should be a bonus."

"My father doesn't think so," Emma said with a grimace. "He hated being called a stepfather—said it made him feel second-rate—so Tommy and I learned not to do that. Just like we remembered to use his name, Smitt, when asked. But he was not pleased to have either of us around. Said we cost too much to feed—even though I never saw him spend a nickel on us."

"Of course," Joshua said. "That's what you said earlier."

"I suppose he did his best," Emma added, although she didn't say it like she believed it.

"Is that what he told you?" Joshua asked.

Emma nodded.

Joshua reached across to pat her hand. "Sometimes people lie."

They were silent for a few minutes.

"I never thought Junior would lie to me," Emma said.

"I won't lie to you," Joshua assured her almost before she finished her sentence.

She glanced up at him, looking startled.

"No one at the ranch will, either," Joshua said, stumbling. "We'll stand by you."

She didn't say anything else.

A good half hour went by before Emma announced that he was to turn right at the next light. They were barely into the outskirts of Missoula. Joshua followed Emma's directions and found himself in a partially industrial area. There were some small businesses and a few used-car dealerships. He could feel her tension increase as they drove closer to where her stepfather was. Joshua thought even Tommy Two was aware of the anxiety since the dog woke up and looked alert.

Joshua gave a glance in the rearview mirror to see that Max was coming along just before Emma held up her hand in a stop signal. Joshua slowed.

"We're here," she said. "The house with the trailer out in front of it is my stepfather's."

Joshua slowed his pickup and parked on the street outside of the small beige frame house. Patches of snow covered the yard, but there was no dead grass on the ground that would have signaled a lawn during the past summer.

"Dirt outside year around," Joshua said.

Emma shrugged. "My stepfather's not one for work."

There was a small rosebush by the front door that hadn't been pruned back so it had bare twigs reaching upward. Matching windows stood on each side of the wooden door.

Joshua noticed Emma looking at a trailer in the driveway to the house.

"That's new," she said.

"I'm guessing it's a rental from the stickers on it," Joshua said.

The trailer carried a full load of boxes and what looked like a headboard and a mattress. There was even a rack of elk horns sticking up from the pile of things.

"It looks like they're moving again," Emma said, her voice heavy with emotion. "He'll say it's to follow the rodeo circuit."

Joshua didn't respond. He didn't have to be a math genius to figure up that Emma's stepfather was a bit old for successful rodeo work. He wondered if the man didn't just dress the part and frequent bars close to the action, hoping for a free drink.

"All the moving is hard on Tommy," Emma said. "He doesn't like to start new schools."

"I can't blame him for that," Joshua said as he parked his pickup behind the trailer and opened his door.

As he walked around to help Emma, he noticed that the snow from yesterday had not been scraped off the concrete slab leading to the house, and as Joshua looked closer, he doubted any snow had been shoveled for the past month. He was careful to keep Emma steady.

When they reached the door, Joshua stepped back so Emma could knock and be the one to enter. He wasn't sure she would want her stepfather to know he was helping her. If so, he would wait outside. Max drove up then and motioned to Joshua that he would stay in his pickup.

A man's voice answered Emma's knock, telling her to come inside. Emma turned the door and opened it.

"Hello?" she called as she entered the house. Her tone sounded tentative, and she reached back to draw Joshua in with her. He was quick to note that while the sunshine was strong, the lights were off, and the heat had apparently been turned off some hours ago.

A woman with dyed red hair stood beside the dining table. She had a mauve and purple knit scarf wrapped around her ears and neck that matched a long purple wool coat. She wore full makeup, lipstick and eyeliner. He'd guess her age at mid-fifties. A few feet away from her was a man, also in a winter jacket and wearing a brown Stetson on his head. He appeared to be a little hungover, or maybe he just had a headache. Joshua got the sense that they had been arguing. No one looked like they'd been hit, though.

"Father," Emma said.

"We're waiting for a phone call," the woman answered.

Joshua glanced over at Emma and saw her face had grown very still as her eyes kept searching for something. "Where's Tommy?"

A low whimper came from the living room area. Joshua looked over and didn't see anyone, but then he saw the dog race behind the couch, and he heard a boy's welcoming giggle.

"Tommy?" Joshua asked, and the giggle ended abruptly like the boy was scared.

"Tommy," Emma echoed in relief as she walked as fast as she could into the living area. She was limping, but she couldn't wait for Joshua. Her heart had been in her throat when she hadn't seen her brother. She remembered the drawing he had made and was afraid her father had sent him ahead somehow. They were clearly moving. At least her father hadn't made Tommy wait out in a cold pickup.

She grabbed Tommy in a big hug, and he rested his head against her shoulder.

"Mommy Two," he whispered. He was near tears.

She started to rub his back when she realized he was still in his pajamas.

"We need to get you dressed," she said as she turned to walk with him back into the dining room. "It's too cold out there to be moving without your winter clothes. Let's get your snowsuit."

Emma looked at her stepfather as she spoke. "Is it in the closet?"

"He outgrew it," Sherry said impatiently. "I gave it away to one of the neighbor kids. They liked the color."

"But Tommy hasn't grown," Emma protested. He was small and had the usual traits of a child with Down syndrome. He was short, with a thick neck that wasn't as long as most and a slightly flatter face than usual. In her eyes, he was beautiful because of his smile.

She looked up at Sherry. "Why did you give his snowsuit away?"

"He wasn't using it," the woman answered, but she looked away as she spoke.

"He does when he goes outside to play," Emma argued.

Sherry looked up at Emma's stepfather. He cleared his throat and spoke, "We decided it's too much for Tommy to go outside."

"Too much to play?" Emma repeated the words in disbelief. "He likes to be with the other children."

Sherry and her stepfather exchanged another look.

"He looks ridiculous out there," Sherry finally spoke, and she sounded angry. "He stumbles and walks slow. Sometimes the other kids tease him. In front of the whole neighborhood. I've never been more uncomfortable in my life than seeing him out there."

Emma gasped. "You were embarrassed. You're keeping him inside because you're embarrassed!"

Emma put Tommy back down on the floor and bent down to speak to him. "Go play with Tommy Two in the living room for a bit."

She waited for the boy and dog to walk into the living room and then she turned back to her stepfather.

"Doesn't the school require him to be outside some? You can't just keep him in the house."

"Sherry isn't comfortable with Tommy," her stepfather said and then had the nerve to smile down at the woman. Then he looked back at Emma. "He isn't even my child, you know. A man shouldn't have someone like Tommy on his back forever just because he'd married the boy's mother at one point. He was not much more than a toddler then, and I didn't know what it would be like. His mother never told me."

"Well, no baby comes with a guarantee. And she can't take him back," Emma pointed out. "She's dead."

"I know but—" Her stepfather started and then just stood there.

Everyone was silent for a moment, and then Joshua walked over and took her hand. She looked up at him and saw her fears confirmed in his face. The coats versus the pajamas told the story. So did that stack of animal-cracker boxes that were the only things on the kitchen counter. Tommy loved those crackers. The cupboard doors were open, and she could see that nothing was left inside.

"You were going to move," Emma accused her stepfather, her voice almost a whisper, "and leave Tommy behind."

Her stepfather kept his eyes on the floor.

"Well, they have homes for children like him," Sherry finally said, with a lift of her head that told everyone she thought she was right. "Him and his Down syndrome."

"Not for seven-year-olds, they don't," Emma protested. "They have some homes for adults, but not for children like Tommy."

"Well, we can't take him with us," Sherry said firmly. "We're going to move to Florida and stay with my sister in that fancy retirement place of hers. I'm sure she doesn't have room for someone like Tommy."

"You can't just leave him," Emma said in a panic, as she looked around. The emptiness of the place finally struck her. "You've even turned the heat off, for goodness sake."

"We were going to call the police when we got an hour or so down the road," her stepfather said, finally raising his eyes defiantly. "He'd be fine until then. They would come and pick him up and take him to a home of some kind. They have to do that—even if it's not a special home. He'd end up somewhere."

Emma sucked in her breath. Somewhere, indeed.

"I won't let that happen," Emma said as she looked up at Joshua. She didn't know what she expected him to do, but she needed help of some sort. Her hand reached into her pocket to grip her grandmother's handkerchief. Joshua's eyes locked with hers at the same time, and she felt that more than the handkerchief steadied her. He had confidence in her.

"I'll take him with me," Emma said as she squared off with her stepfather. She didn't expect him to allow that, either.

Her stepfather surprised her, because he glanced down at Sherry.

"Babe?" he asked.

"I don't care," she told him. "Just as long as I don't have to look at his face any longer."

"I'll even make it legal," her stepfather said as he darted into another room and came back with a piece of paper, a pen and a business envelope. He wrote a few sentences on the paper and with a flourish folded the page and slid it into the envelope, sealing it.

"Here you go," her stepfather said as he held out the envelope to Emma. "You'll regret it, no doubt, but it will be too late by then. He's all yours."

Emma snatched the envelope from him and called for Tommy.

"Emma will want to send you a postcard," Joshua said to her stepfather. "Ask how your trip was. That kind of thing. You going to end up around Orlando?"

"Miami," her stepfather said. "Close to the beach."

"At the Exclusive Royal Beach Retirement Home," Sherry added proudly. "It's very impressive. My sister, Amelia Dawson, owns there. Golf courses and all of that. And a theater. Imagine. You can even take cruises from there—well, you take a bus to the dock, but still—"

"Sounds great," Joshua said.

Emma looked at Joshua in disbelief. This was no time for polite chitchat.

Her stepfather's face relaxed. "You'll have to come see us some time."

"But—" Sherry protested before stopping when her stepfather gave her a look.

"Well," Emma stood there trying to think of something appropriate to say, but there was nothing that wasn't rude so she said it again. "Well."

It was apparently enough, because her stepfather gave her a nod.

Joshua stood as if to guard her while she called out to Tommy. Her brother and his dog came quickly.

"My brother needs his winter coat," Emma said to her stepfather only to see him give a shrug.

"Don't tell me you gave that away, too?" she asked.

"Sold it," Sherry answered smugly. "Got a good price, too. I figured they'd have those kinds of things where he was going."

"A blanket, then," Emma suggested, barely restraining her temper. Had they given away or sold all of Tommy's things? It appeared so. Maybe that's why he'd asked her to keep his drawings and Tommy Two.

"Here," her stepfather said as he took off his jacket and, over Sherry's objections, gave it to Emma. It was far too big for the boy, but Emma scooped him up as best she could with the bump of her pregnancy and wrapped the coat around him. Then she let Joshua guide them out of the house. She didn't even remember that her ankle hurt until Joshua came beside her to steady her arm.

"Thank you," she said as she looked up at him.

"He's an armful," Joshua said with a nod at her brother.

She was glad for the coat as Tommy snuggled down inside of it. She didn't know what Tommy had understood about what their stepfather had planned or what he would think about living with her.

Then he reached a small hand up to her face and touched her. "I go with Mommy Two," he said and gave his crooked little smile. "Me happy."

"I'm happy, too," Emma whispered and bent down to kiss his face.

By that time, they were at Joshua's pickup, and he opened the passenger door for them. Joshua held out his arms for Tommy, and Emma gave her brother to him.

"Why don't you sit in the middle?" Joshua suggested

to Emma. "That way the boy can enjoy being with his dog."

Emma nodded. Her brother would like that.

She climbed into the pickup and slid to the middle. Joshua handed Tommy inside, and the boy sat next to her. And then the dog jumped up and sat at Tommy's feet.

"What should I tell Max?" Joshua asked as he stood outside the open door.

"Tell him we're going home," she said. "I miss my mountain."

Joshua was silent for a moment. "I think you need to come to the ranch."

"But—" Emma started to protest when Joshua interrupted.

"You're going to have to stay with us at the ranch until you have the baby at least," Joshua said quietly. "You can't expect the boy to take care of you in a situation like that. He'd be scared, and it's not fair to make him run down to get Max. It's too far."

Emma closed her eyes. He was right. She hadn't thought about that.

"I don't want Bailey to take care of me," she finally admitted. Junior's real wife was a good woman. But Emma had spent her life giving forced smiles to women doling out charity to her, from food-bank workers to clothing-drive volunteers. She did not want to start her new life with her baby that way.

"There's a room—the foreman's room—in the bunkhouse that you can have," Joshua said. "It's got its own bathroom and a small kitchen. Your brother and Max, if he comes, can have a bunk in the main part where Mark Dakota—he's the other ranch hand—

and I sleep. Don't worry about Mark. He's a good guy, and he likes kids. We have six bunks in that area so we have plenty of room. And Bailey Rosen doesn't even come into the bunkhouse unless there's something wrong that needs fixing. She recently got the bunkhouse set up with a propane-heating stove so it's nice and warm, too."

Emma nodded wearily. She had no other choice. She hadn't even thought about how she would get enough wood to keep the temperature in the trailer warm enough for the baby. "Okay, then."

"I'll go talk to Max." Joshua stepped back and closed the door. "I think he'll come, too."

Emma sat in the cab, breathing in the smell of wet dog and electric heat, and wondered what she had just done. The only one who had ever offered her a place to stay had been Junior. Pity hadn't been what motivated him. He had married her. Having Tommy with her changed everything, though. And soon there would be the baby. She wondered if maybe she should offer to pay rent for that room in the bunkhouse.

"Me hungry," her brother whispered as Joshua's door opened.

"Did you have breakfast?" Emma asked.

Her brother shook his head.

"We'll pull over, and I'll get us some hamburgers or something," Joshua said as he put the key into the pickup's ignition and turned it. The purr of the engine sounded strong and steady. "Max is coming, too."

"I'll pay for the hamburgers," Emma said softly.

"Don't be silly," Joshua protested. "I can pay."

Emma shook her head. "Not today. I insist."

Joshua didn't say anything after that, but when they

got to the drive-through window, he let her pay for the hamburgers on the condition that he pay for milkshakes to go with them. Emma thanked him as she tucked her change back into her wallet. She did not mind sharing the cost with someone; she just didn't want charity. She wished her mother and grandmother could have seen her paying her own way, at least partially.

"Did your family ever have to take charity?" Emma asked, suddenly curious. She had a feeling the two of them were more alike than Joshua had said.

"That wasn't our problem," Joshua said as he pulled into a parking space on the street beside the diner. "No matter how drunk my father would get, he always sobered up enough to do his job at the liquor store. They didn't seem to mind if he smelled of whiskey."

Joshua turned the ignition off and handed Emma and Tommy each a wrapped hamburger. Max pulled up behind them. He had his own meal.

"Your home life wasn't so bad, then," Emma murmured as she started to unwrap the food.

Joshua looked over at her in surprise, a flash of something racing across his face before it disappeared and his features became orderly again. "I wouldn't say that. My sister—"

He stopped and set his hamburger on the dashboard.

Emma waited for him to continue. "What happened to your sister?"

He was silent for so long she thought he wasn't going to respond. "It's okay."

She didn't want to force him to tell her anything, but then he did.

Chapter Four

Joshua forced himself to tell Emma his worst secret. His voice came out flat and strained. "My sister was eight years old and cut her arm on an old metal swing in our yard. I was two years younger than her, and she used to push me high in that swing. One day a bar broke off suddenly, and it was jagged on the end. She reached up to stop the bar from hitting me, and it hit her instead."

"She sounds like a very caring sister," Emma said quietly.

Joshua nodded and took a breath. He'd never told anyone this before, and he had to search for the words. "It made a bad cut on her arm. We knew our father would be upset—he got mad at everything—so my sister didn't tell him or our mother. She wrapped a dish towel around it so our parents didn't notice the cut, and it was getting more and more infected. I didn't see that, either, until my sister got sick, and finally she asked me to go tell one of our neighbors. I was shy, though, so I went and told our father instead. He promised he'd see to it, but he didn't do anything. My sister died the next day."

"Oh," Emma breathed out the word. "I'm so sorry."

"She trusted me, and I let her down," Joshua said. He'd said the whole story and didn't feel any better for it.

"But you were only six years old," Emma said.

"I was all she had," Joshua said. "Even the social worker who took me away from my parents said it was too bad I hadn't gone for help. In my mind, I had gone for help. To my father."

Joshua let the silence settle upon the cab of his pickup. Tommy was sitting by the window, and he was quietly eating his hamburger. Next to him Emma hadn't moved since he'd started talking.

"That's why you're helping me, isn't it?" Emma finally said.

"I don't know." Joshua looked down at her. "But it could be."

Emma nodded and seemed to consider that. "So, I'm kind of like a sister to you?"

"No," Joshua said firmly without even thinking.

"I see," Emma said, her voice flat. "I'm sure she was special."

Joshua reached over and traced Emma's jawline with his thumb. "You're special, too. That's why you're not like a sister to me."

Emma smiled slightly at that, and Joshua felt his mood lift.

"We better eat these hamburgers," Joshua said and looked across the seat. "Your brother's already done."

"Me ate it," Tommy confirmed as he crumpled up the wrapper as evidence.

A half hour later, Joshua reached up to touch the brim of his hat and found that it was still damp after the snowflakes had melted. He'd taken if off to eat his hamburger but had put it back on a few minutes ago. The heater was pushing out enough warm air to make the cab comfortable, even though the rhythm of the wipers proved there was still a steady drip of cold moisture on the windshield. Looking over at Emma, he noticed her coat had dark wet patches on it, too. The dog was snoring lightly at her feet, and the boy had his face burrowed into the crook of Emma's elbow, his body tucked under his stepfather's jacket.

Joshua put the key in the ignition and started the engine. Then he pulled back onto the main street, Max following behind him.

The smell of grilled hamburgers filled the pickup, and they'd crumpled up the empty wrappers before putting them, along with the milkshake cups, in a brown paper bag that sat on the seat. The boy hadn't wanted anyone to throw the wrappers away, and Joshua saw no need to try and change his mind. He seemed to like the bright colors and the numbers on them. Joshua didn't know much about Down syndrome, but he could already tell that Tommy was a good boy who didn't ask much from life.

"We're going to need to stop and get some clothes for the boy," he said. They were on the outskirts of Missoula and would soon head east on Interstate 90. "There are a couple of small towns ahead."

"I wonder if they have any stores for children's clothes," Emma answered. "Most small towns don't."

"We have a closet with some stray clothing at the

ranch," Joshua offered. "But I don't think there's anything small enough for the boy."

"His name is Tommy," Emma said, her voice tight.

"I know," Joshua replied. "It's just—" He faltered. He wasn't sure how to explain it, and then he saw Tommy turn his head enough to almost peek out at him. Even then he focused on Joshua's shoulder. And, as with the request for the food wrappers, Tommy never really looked at him. "I thought he might be shy. I wasn't sure he'd like me to use his name."

"Oh." Emma sounded surprised. "It's true; he is shy, but…" She shifted so she could see her brother's face. "Is it okay if Joshua calls you Tommy?"

The boy's small shoulders shrugged, but he did finally turn around and look more directly at him. Joshua almost said something to Tommy, but then he saw fear in the young boy's eyes. Maybe it wasn't shyness that stopped him, Joshua thought as the boy slid even closer to Emma.

"Is he mad at me?" Tommy whispered to Emma as he pointed at Joshua.

Joshua figured he wasn't supposed to hear the question, but he answered anyway. "I'm not at all mad at you."

Joshua barely got his words out before Tommy started to shake.

Emma scooped the boy up into her arms. "It's okay," she said as she rubbed her brother's back. "It's okay. You're safe with us. No one's mad at you."

Tommy gave a low moan as he rocked himself in her arms. The sound woke up the dog, and the animal started to howl.

Joshua put a hand inside his coat to feel his front

shirt pocket. Sometimes he had wrapped hard candies in there for the stray niece or nephew, but there were none today. He did feel the earring that was still tucked in the corner, but now wasn't the time for that either. He looked across at Emma. "Kids like me. Really, they do. I'm uncle to a lot of them. A favorite uncle."

He checked the pocket of his coat to see if he had a biscuit for the dog at least. He did not. Then he looked over at Emma.

"It's okay," she responded in much the same tone she had used to soothe Tommy. "Some of us just don't trust strangers as much as we should."

Joshua nodded and remembered the boy had been hiding behind a sofa when he met him. Maybe it just took him time to warm up to someone new. He checked his rearview mirror to be sure Max was following along behind them. It was probably a good thing the older man was going with them to the ranch. Tommy seemed to like him.

Joshua looked ahead and saw an exit sign for a town. "Should we stop for a break?"

Emma nodded, and Joshua set his turn signal to blinking. He figured they could all use a quick walk around the pickup even if there was nothing much else to do in the place.

The town was covered with snowdrifts; even the trees were layered with glittering white frost. A plow had gone down the main street and made everything look like a postcard. Several of the businesses were open, a hardware store and an antique shop. Joshua pulled into the only gas station he could see. He parked under a wide overhang where the concrete had been scraped clean of ice. At least there would be restrooms to use here.

He watched Max pull in behind him. Since the overhang would prevent the snow from falling on them as they walked into the station, Joshua took off his Stetson, setting it on the dash in front of the steering wheel. He would let it sit there and dry some more. By then he realized Emma was trying to get Tommy ready for going outside.

"I forgot he doesn't have any shoes," Joshua said as he saw the boy's bare toes sticking out of the coat wrapped around him.

Emma glanced up and nodded. "He used to have sneakers at least. His feet are wide, and it's hard to find shoes to fit."

"Red lights on my shoes," Tommy looked over and informed Joshua. The boy's fear appeared to have vanished even though he did look mournful. "Gone."

"Maybe we'll find another pair for you." The minute he saw the excitement leap up in Tommy's eyes, Joshua knew he shouldn't have made the offer. "Not today, I don't think," Joshua added quickly. There would be no shoes in the stores they saw in front of them. "But soon," he said with more confidence. He could drive into Miles City tomorrow. "I'm not sure I can find red lights on them, but I'll do my best. We'll have to draw an outline, a picture of your foot, and I can take it with me when I go shopping."

Joshua didn't want Emma out shopping and didn't know if her brother would go without her.

Tommy was looking at his foot dubiously. It was wider and flatter than most feet. Joshua wondered if the feet were that way to match the short, stocky look of the boy's body.

"Me draw no feet," Tommy said finally.

"I'm sure you can," Emma said encouragingly. "You can draw a picture of anything."

Tommy gave a quiet smile, and Joshua could tell he was pleased.

"What your stepfather did should be criminal," Joshua muttered to Emma, his voice low enough that Tommy wouldn't hear. "Even a child is entitled to own his shoes."

"New shoes for me," Tommy said emphatically, still celebrating the earlier conversation.

Joshua grinned. "You've got it. Maybe tomorrow."

Tommy smiled a little wider this time.

Emma started to zip up the coat over Tommy's pajamas. She had pulled the wool scarf out of the glove compartment. "We can wrap this around his feet."

Joshua nodded. "It will at least keep his toes warm."

"Toes need shoes," Tommy said and then giggled.

Joshua chuckled with him. "They sure do, champ."

"Me champ?" Tommy asked eagerly.

Joshua nodded. "You sure are."

Tommy grinned. "Champ needs shoes."

Emma kept moving Tommy around in her arms and finally Joshua realized it would be difficult for her to carry him being as pregnant as she was. He guessed it was her anger that made her able to do it at her stepfather's place.

"I could carry him on my back," Joshua offered.

"Piggyback?" Tommy asked as his face beamed.

"Did your stepfather let you ride piggyback?" Joshua asked, surprised that the boy even knew what it was.

Tommy frowned and shook his head.

Joshua nodded, wondering what kind of a man their stepfather had been not to open up his heart to this tenderhearted young boy.

"It was Junior that taught him to ride like that," Emma said quietly.

Joshua had to hide his shock. He wouldn't have credited his old boss with that kind of kindness to anyone.

Joshua didn't know how to respond so he just climbed out of the pickup and walked around to the passenger door. Tommy climbed right up on his back, and Emma pulled the coat up over his head.

A few wet snowflakes hit Joshua as he raced to the gas station's store with the boy clinging to his back. Joshua could see that Max had parked behind them, and he motioned for the man to come around and help Emma walk into the store.

By the time they got inside, Tommy was holding on to fistfuls of Joshua's hair in a bid to keep his balance. The boy must have enjoyed his ride if his squeals were any indication.

"How did you like your horseback ride?" Joshua asked as he twisted to lift Tommy down on to the station's linoleum floor.

"Piggyback ride," Tommy corrected him.

Joshua nodded. "Right you are."

Emma and Max came into the store at that moment and Joshua noted that the four of them almost filled up the small space the store had in front of the counter.

A tall thin man in a ponytail stood behind the counter watching them as they all looked around.

"Reggie!" Max said suddenly and stepped toward the counter. "Remember me? I didn't know your station was around here. We met at that conference a few years ago in Bozeman for independent gas-station owners."

"Max!" the man shouted out and walked from behind the counter to thump Max on the back.

"Good to see you, Max," Reggie said. His narrow face was grinning. "What brings you down from that station of yours? I figured you were a hermit up there."

Max puffed out his chest slightly. "I get around."

"I guess so," Reggie said. "Where's that bird of yours? What was his name? Valentine? No, Cupid."

"Yup, Cupid it is," Max said. "He's out in my pickup with his shade down."

"I'll send a bag of peanuts out to him," Reggie said and then asked, "How can I help you all today?"

"We're looking for some clothes for the boy here," Max pointed at Tommy. "Even some shoes if you have them."

"Here?" Reggie said. "I don't run to that kind of merchandise. Don't even have a T-shirt, and I know lots of stations carry local ones."

"Aw," said Max. "Too bad. No flip-flops or anything?"

Reggie shook his head. "The closest I come is a few costumes left over from the holidays. I thought I'd try them out last year. Sold quite a few, too."

Max looked over at Emma who passed the look on to Joshua.

"What do you think, Tommy?" Joshua asked.

The boy shrugged but didn't seem distressed at the idea.

"Are they plastic?" Joshua asked.

Reggie shrugged. "No, cloth mostly. There's a couple that would keep the boy warmer than those pajamas he has on. It can be pretty cold in Montana. If you want them you can have them. I've been thinking of tossing them since I don't plan to offer costumes any longer."

Joshua glanced over at Emma, and she nodded.

Reggie went into a back room and came out with several costumes. They took a pumpkin costume, with *Thankful* written on it, because it was made out of a heavy orange quilted material that would be warm, and Tommy said orange was good. Then Reggie suggested a Christmas-elf costume.

"And it has those elf slippers," Reggie noted like a true salesman. "The boy can use those for his feet. There's even a little bell on the part that points up."

"Bell," Tommy repeated as Reggie folded the costumes and handed them to the boy.

Joshua bought everyone their own bag of nuts and a large ice tea, slipping the store owner an extra twenty-dollar bill in the process.

"Thanks," Joshua whispered.

"He looks like a good kid," the man said.

They walked outside and climbed into their respective pickups.

"That was fun," Emma said when she and Tommy were settled into Joshua's vehicle again. She pulled out her wallet and passed several bills to Joshua. "I saw what you did, and I approve, but I'm the one who should be wearing the pumpkin costume. It would fit, at least."

Joshua chuckled as he passed the bills back. "It was a reward to that man for having a good heart. No charge to you. The peanuts are on me."

Then he plucked his Stetson off the dashboard and

put it back on his head. "I'm guessing most pregnant women feel like pumpkins by this time."

Joshua looked over to share the laugh with Emma and was taken back to see the look on Tommy's face. He had been so cheerful when they stopped, and now he was shrinking away from Joshua and looking at him with fear.

"What's the matter, champ?" Joshua said softly.

The boy started to cry.

Joshua looked to Emma for help. "I don't know what I did wrong."

"Nothing," she whispered as her brother squeezed as close to her as he could get in his pumpkin costume.

"We can switch you back to your pajamas," Joshua offered.

Tommy didn't seem to want that, but Joshua didn't know what else to do. Finally, Emma draped the coat over the boy's head and that seemed to calm him.

"Do you want to ride the rest of the way with Max?" Joshua asked, even though he feared the answer.

Emma shook her head. "I think we'll be fine now."

Joshua nodded and turned on the ignition. He was glad that she was willing to stay with him, but he had no idea what he was doing wrong. One minute Tommy was afraid of him, and the next he was riding piggyback into the store. And when they came back to the pickup, he was terrified again.

Joshua drove back toward the entrance to the freeway.

"Is he upset in small spaces?" Joshua looked across to Emma. The cab was pretty confined, especially with three people and a dog inside it.

"I don't know," Emma whispered. "There's so much I don't know."

"But you love him, anyway," Joshua said.

She nodded. "One of the reasons I married Junior was that he said Tommy could come live with us when we got settled ourselves."

"Hmm." Joshua didn't know what to say to that so he just kept his mouth shut and his speed low as he drove back onto Interstate 90. Then he glanced over and saw Emma. The weary pain on her face was almost his undoing.

"I have a box," he said impulsively, wanting to do whatever he could to erase the worry lines on her face. "It might help."

"What kind of a box would that be?" she said lightly as though he was suggesting a word game.

"A cigar box," he answered. "With a golden palm tree on the top." He took a risk. "It's full of lots of money."

"Oh," she said brightly. "I love find-the-treasure games. Do I ask questions?"

"You can," he said, knowing he had at least distracted her from her troubles for a time.

"Is it bigger than a bread box?" she asked.

"No," Joshua said.

"Is it in a different state?" she asked.

"No," he said, smiling this time.

Emma kept asking questions, and Joshua kept answering them, but she got no closer to the knowledge of where that cigar box of money actually was. He knew she'd be shocked if he pulled it out, anyway. It was all imaginary to her. Long pauses came between the questions now, and they stopped for tacos at another fast-food restaurant. They ate in the truck, not sure if the world was ready for a Pumpkin Tommy yet. The sun was setting, and what clouds they could see were rimmed with gold. Emma asked if the cigar box full of cash was at the end of the rainbow. Tommy giggled at that one, and it made Joshua's heart feel good to hear him. He noticed the boy didn't turn around so he could see him, however.

At some point, Tommy fell asleep, and the dog stopped twitching in his nap. Not much snow fell, and Joshua was at peace. He liked the sound of Emma's voice as she made her guesses. After a time, her questions stopped completely, and he looked over to see her eyelids drooping.

She must have sensed him glancing over at her because she put her head up. "I'm awake."

"You don't need to be," Joshua said. "You've had a long day. Take a nap if you want. I'll wake you when we get home—uh, to the ranch."

"Someone needs to keep a lookout," she said with a slight shake of her head.

"You don't trust me?" Joshua asked.

"I don't trust any man," she said firmly. "Especially when they're driving."

Joshua didn't respond for a few minutes, and then he said softly, "You must have trusted Junior."

"Junior doesn't count," she told him a little too quickly, he thought.

"He counted enough for you to marry him," Joshua said, trying not to sound indignant.

"Junior was good to me," Emma said carefully. Joshua almost interrupted her with a protest, but he restrained himself.

"He respected me," Emma said. "I know that. I was a waitress where he ate. Every day for a week he came in and had a deluxe hamburger and a piece of pie. And a cup of coffee."

"That sounds like Junior," Joshua admitted. Junior never had spent much time on the ranch, even though his wife, Bailey, and their daughter, Rosie, lived there.

"I didn't know he was married," Emma said quietly. "I wouldn't have talked with him so much if I had."

Joshua grunted. "I expect most folks know you're not to blame in this. We all know it was Junior's fault."

"My mother once told me I should never trust a man who wanted to give me too much money," Emma said thoughtfully. "I thought about that with Junior. She said the honest ones would offer me a small diamond and not cash—that the cash was either charity or came from bad motives."

Joshua gulped. He was glad that cigar box was securely lodged under his seat. "Not all money is suspect."

Emma rolled her eyes at him. "It is when it's coming from a man. Even from a woman my mother felt cash gifts robbed a person of their pride. She never wanted cash charity."

"Well." Joshua was speechless. If he ever needed a glib tongue it was now, but he didn't have anything to say.

"Junior gave me the earrings," Emma said softly. "Two small dangling diamonds on each one. He said they were worth a thousand for each diamond, but he made me promise I would never sell them. They were for me to enjoy so it wasn't like they were cash. He said he'd get me the diamond ring later, but those earrings were how I knew he cared about me. I'm afraid someone stole one of the earrings," Emma finally noted sadly, and Joshua's heart dropped. Then she continued. "I keep the other one with my marriage papers. When I get a little ahead with some money, I plan to have an earring made to match the one I have so I will have the pair of them again. If I can ever afford it, that is."

Joshua had never thought he was a coward, but he would rather have waved a white flag than tell her. "I have it," he managed to croak out.

"You have my earring?" she looked up in the shadows. He could not see the expression on her face or in her eyes, only shapes in the darkness. "How is that even possible?"

He cleared his throat. "I didn't take it. You lost it by the car when I tried to open the door for you that day at Eli's funeral."

"Oh," she said, still sounding a little puzzled.

"It's in my shirt pocket right now," he said. "I'll dig it out for you when we get home. I told the attorney about it the next day. You can ask him when we get to the ranch. I wasn't keeping it secret. He must not have given you the message."

"Well," she said and paused. "Thank you. I guess I'm too suspicious. I'm glad you found it. That will save me paying for having another one made. Besides, it will be the one that Junior gave me, and that makes it special."

"I suppose," Joshua managed. He had a hard time getting on the Junior bandwagon.

"I know you don't think so, but Junior was kind to me," Emma continued and looked away. "He came by one of my tables so often that, one day, I started to tell him what was happening at home. Tommy's mother had died, and my stepfather was giving me the creeps." Emma looked up. "I hadn't worked long enough to get my own apartment, and there was Tommy. I managed to dodge my stepfather, but—"

Emma looked out the side window of the pickup and stared into the darkness.

They were both quiet for a time.

"I didn't know that was the situation," Joshua finally said.

Emma didn't answer. Shortly after, she dozed off. He looked over at her now and again, just to check on her. It made no sense for him to care for her as much as he did. She wasn't his sister, but he was glad that he was able to help her. If he wasn't mistaken, he halfway even trusted her. He wondered what the future would hold for them.

Emma woke up in darkness. The air was damp, but she didn't notice it at first because her cheek was resting against the closed window of the pickup, and the glass was cold. She shifted, and Tommy, who was burrowed into her side, moved with her slightly. The dog was moving around at her feet. It took her a minute or so to realize the pickup was no longer moving.

"Are we there?" she mumbled as she looked over at the silhouette of Joshua on the other side of the seat. His hat was tipped so she couldn't see the contours of his face, except for a portion of his chin. He did have a fine jawline, she thought, but then wondered if it wasn't just because he seemed so determined.

"I was just going to wake you up," Joshua said, his voice low as he turned to her. He pushed his Stetson farther back on his head, and she could almost see his eyes. She didn't say anything.

"I looked down the road and saw that Max is coming," he said. "So, I'm waiting to be sure he makes the turn here. All of the other vehicles are here—that includes Mark's. Remember I told you he's the other ranch hand? And, well, he and Bailey are courting—I suppose that's you would call it."

"Like dating?" Emma exclaimed. "But Junior's only been dead a month!"

She was shocked, and then she corrected herself. "Well, maybe it's been a few weeks longer, but still."

Joshua shrugged. "I don't know how long a person is supposed to mourn. Especially when their spouse had played them false for years."

"Junior and I didn't even know each other for years," Emma protested fiercely. "That can't be right. He didn't play her false for longer than a year. That's it."

She refused to be the excuse Bailey used for not mourning Junior.

Joshua was silent for a minute and then said, "There were others—before you. Not that Junior even pretended to marry any of the others. Or had children with them."

"Oh," Emma said.

"And Mark and Bailey go way back," Joshua continued. "Knew each other as kids. I worked on the ranch and knew them then, too. Bailey was always sweet on Mark. She'd follow him around and chat with him while he worked."

Emma nodded. She felt foolish; the two of them sounded like friends. "I hope she'll find happiness with him, then."

Joshua looked toward the house. "The rest of the people on the ranch must be asleep. And no wonder, as late as it is."

Joshua smiled across the seat to Emma. "Welcome to the Rosen Ranch," he said with a flourish in his voice.

Emma glanced out the side and back windows. She couldn't even see all of the property, but she knew it was huge.

"I can understand why everyone was shocked when I refused to consider claiming part of this," she said. The ranch could be on one of those television shows; it was that impressive.

Joshua smiled. "It's big and in good shape. Worth owning, that's for sure."

Emma nodded in response. She felt overwhelmed. Junior had always spoken of them remodeling and living in the trailer, and he had put the deed for that land and structure in her name. They were going to raise those Alpine goats for their milk and maybe get some llamas to sell. That had been the independence she wanted. She could pay her own way.

In the moonlight, she looked further out over the fields. She counted at least six, or maybe it was eight, buildings. A classic red barn with a hayloft and a large fenced corral. Several round silos. Two rectangular buildings with doors high enough to store tractors. An assortment of what looked like small toolsheds— or maybe one of them was a chicken coop. Tall trees framed a white ranch house that had a comfortable porch in the front and a screened side porch on the left.

A layer of snow covered everything, but she could see the outlines of several flower beds. Nothing was blooming, of course, but she could see the pruned rose-bushes and the level spaces where other flowers had been. Someone in that house had taken care to make it a home. A child's wagon with two red balls in it was pulled up to the front porch. Tommy would love to play with that, she thought, as she turned her attention back to the cab of the pickup.

This ranch was fifty times better than her dream of the mountain trailer. She wondered if Junior would have come to live with her in that trailer, after all. Probably not even for a few months, she decided.

She supposed it was Bailey, the woman who was Junior's real wife, who had made this place into a home. Emma had seen her at the funeral, but she hadn't expected to meet her again. Her flash of an impression had been of a strong, forthright woman who spoke her mind. She'd been pretty, too.

Emma finally realized Joshua had been peering into the darkness for some time now. She wondered if he was giving her time to get used to being on the ranch. It was a different world than she was used to, that was for sure.

"I didn't want Tommy's dog to start barking before I could see where Rosie's dog, Guard, is sleeping," he said, though, and she decided maybe that was all he had been doing. Maybe it was not obvious to him that she was out of her league here.

"Isn't Rosie the little girl?" Emma stretched as she asked the question. She supposed she would have to acknowledge some of the people at this place. She could start with the girl. "What's she doing with a dog named Guard?"

"Our little Rosie is something. You might think she's

a princess with all of her fairy tales, but she's really more interested in dragons than in fancy dresses. She could command an army if she had one—and she'd like to have one. I've seen her trying to herd a bunch of chickens like they were military troops, and she almost kept them in line. As it is, she reminds her dog that he's her royal guard and must do what she says. I must admit he does better than the chickens."

"She sounds charming." Emma turned and started to figure out how to move her brother. He felt like a sack of flour leaning against her. "What child doesn't want to have the world run the way they want?"

"Let me help you with the boy," Joshua said as he opened his door.

"Thank you," Emma muttered softly.

Joshua opened her door carefully and then looked straight up. "There's a full moon tonight."

Emma smiled. That was why there was a soft glow over everything. "My mother used to call it a lover's moon. I always figured it was more of a troublemaker's moon, though—light enough to get into mischief."

Looking at the moon had been one of her good memories of her mother. In years past, Emma used to watch the moon and talk to her mother, pretending she was still alive.

Joshua chuckled as he helped Emma step down from the cab. "I'll carry Tommy inside. Hopefully, he won't wake up and be scared."

Emma shook her head. "I don't know why he seemed frightened today. He was doing fine with you, and then, all of a sudden, he wasn't."

"Well, he's had a long day," Joshua said. "I'm guessing he was all keyed-up about your stepfather moving. I wonder if he sensed he was going to be left behind."

Emma shrugged. "Probably. Tommy's not the best at school, but he can usually figure things out pretty well when he needs to."

Joshua gently reached in and gathered Tommy up into his arms. Then they started toward the building in front of them.

"We'll get you settled in the bunkhouse and worry about introductions in the morning," Joshua said. "The foreman's suite has been empty for a year or so now. The man's wife used to stay over with him some-times—they had a house in Miles City—but she fig-ured the foreman's quarters should be a little fancier than the rest of the bunkhouse. So, I hope it will be okay. We never go in there."

Joshua had Tommy halfway slung over one shoulder. He offered the other elbow to Emma. She took it, and they began to walk toward the bunkhouse. The building was painted white like the house and had a fair number of windows. A layer of snow covered the wide porch.

"I'll pay you for use of the room," Emma said.

Joshua looked down. "You're our guest."

"I was just missing my mother," Emma said. "She would have wanted me to pay my way."

Joshua put his arm around her shoulder. "I'm sorry she's not with you, but I think she'd understand. We need to think about the baby."

"I suppose," Emma added as she turned a little to capture more of Joshua's loose hug. They made a group with Tommy slung over one of Joshua's shoulders and her leaning into the other.

Joshua reached out and opened the door. He took

the first step inside, and Emma followed. It was darker in the large room than it was outside, and it smelled musty. When Joshua flipped a light switch the area became visible. Single beds lined the walls along three sides. She counted six beds. Two of them looked like they were being used. The others had sheets on them, but no blankets.

The sound of an engine grew louder outside.

"That'll be Max," Joshua said as he walked over and laid Tommy down on one of the unclaimed beds. "I'll go outside so he can see where to park."

Before Joshua left the main room, he nodded to a door on the far wall. "That leads to the foreman's suite. I'd suggest leaving the door open so the room gets some heat. It's got a private bathroom in there. And a small kitchen fixed up along one wall. Feel free to make tea or whatever you find back there."

With that, Joshua opened the door to the outside, stepped through and closed it.

Emma looked over to see that Tommy was still sleeping. She decided she would take a peek at where she was going to be staying before she put Tommy to bed.

When she opened the door, she saw shadows around the foreman's room that were cast by the light in the main room. A big rug was spread over the first half of the room. A comfortable-looking recliner sat beside a small table, and a pole lamp at the edge of the rug. In the back half of the room, there was a full bed, pushed square against the wall and topped by a quilt made of satin squares, some of which were covered with lace. The shine of the satin reflected back and made it look old-fashioned and fanciful. Two white fluffy pillows sat at the top of the bed.

Stepping back into the main part of the bunkhouse, she went to Tommy's bed and took off his pumpkin costume. He was already in his pajamas, and he didn't stir when she rolled him between the sheets. Then she looked around for some blankets and saw several on a shelf along one wall. She unfolded two of the blankets and spread them over Tommy. Then she bent down and kissed him lightly on the forehead. He didn't wake up, but she knew there was nothing he liked more than receiving a kiss.

She stood there watching her brother sleep. They had both had a big day. She had never expected to be solely responsible for him, but she wasn't sorry she'd told their stepfather that she would care for Tommy.

She wished he could tell her what had frightened him. Now that they were alone, she could admit that she wondered if he saw something in Joshua that she didn't see yet. Tommy had good instincts about people. Today he'd looked at Joshua the same way he used to look at their stepfather. She'd seen no indication that the kind of meanness her stepfather showed was part of Joshua, but Tommy might be a better judge of that than she was.

The door opened right then, and Joshua and Max stepped inside. The older man was carrying a duffel bag in one hand and Cupid's cage in the other. Tommy's dog slipped in behind them. Fortunately, the covering was on the cage, and the bird seemed to be asleep.

Emma wondered suddenly why Max had a duffel.

"Did you know we'd be coming to the ranch?" she asked the older man.

"I always keep a bag in my pickup," Max explained with a shake of his head as he set the bird cage on a small side table. "Ready for adventures and all that."

"Oh," Emma said. "I would never think to—" She gave a small laugh. "I didn't even bring a toothbrush."

"We have some new ones in a drawer over here," Joshua said as he walked over to a small bureau. "Toothpaste, too, and several brands. Small bottles of shampoo, too. Take your pick."

Joshua held out several packaged toothbrushes and unopened tubes of toothpaste. "Here. Take what you need for Tommy, too."

"Thank you," Emma said as she picked the items she and her brother could use. She wondered about Tommy's intuition. Her stepfather would never think to offer anyone a new toothbrush, mostly because he would never consider or care what someone else would need.

She turned to glance at Max. The older man was studying the room and nodding.

"Well, we made it," Max declared in a hearty voice. "This here is a palace compared to places I've slept over the years."

"At least it has good propane heat in this room," Joshua said, satisfaction in his voice. "Just pick out your bunk and find some blankets. The other ranch hand, Mark, is sleeping in the barn tonight. We have a heifer that's ready to calf, and there's a cot out there. He stepped out to tell me that Bailey had her baby—a girl. And Mark and Bailey are now officially engaged, or next thing to it. Hallelujah, I say to that. Mrs. Hargrove, who's like a grandmother to everyone in Dry

Creek, has been sharing a room with Rosie so she'll be on hand to help Bailey and the baby for a few days."

Emma smiled. "The baby is well?"

"Perfect, according to Mark," Joshua said with a grin. "That man was bursting his buttons—as proud as any real father would have been. He must have thumped me on the back a half-dozen times."

Max walked over to one of the beds and set his duffel on the floor beside it.

Emma kept the smile on her face, but she felt the tightness in her chest. She didn't know who would be happy when her baby was born. Of course, she would be, but it would be nice to have her baby celebrated by more than one person.

"Find everything?" Joshua asked her.

Emma nodded. "Tommy should be fine. He usually sleeps through the night, and he's tired enough to do that and more."

She looked over and noted that Tommy's dog had curled up beside his bunk.

"I'll keep an eye on your brother," Joshua assured her. "And if he needs you, you're right next door."

"Thanks," she said as she started walking to the door. "I think I will leave the door open, though, for the heat."

"Night, night," Joshua said softly, and he smiled when she turned back to look at him in surprise.

"That's for the baby," Joshua explained. "So the little one knows they have a friend on the outside waiting for them while they're doing their time."

"Oh," Emma said with a shake of her head. "What do you mean, *doing their time*? It's not like the baby's in jail."

Joshua just grinned.

"Besides, this baby doesn't even know you," Emma said as she opened the door. "So it can't be your friend."

"But I can be their friend," Joshua replied, and she looked back to see him standing there looking a little wistful. "I can't wait to meet the little one."

She didn't know what to say, but she didn't want him to know his words touched her. "Well, you won't meet my baby tonight so you can relax."

Then Emma walked through the door into her own private room. Knowing she was alone, she felt fatigue settle on her like a heavy blanket. That man's words shouldn't have brought a lump to her throat, but they did. He was only talking nonsense, she told herself, like men did sometimes. She needed to forget it. She'd wash up and brush her teeth, and then she'd slip into that bed. As she walked closer to the bed, she saw the edges of ivory satin sheets peeking out from under the quilt.

"It is a palace," she whispered, thinking of what Max had said. She'd never slept on satin sheets before. A few minutes later, she felt the luxury of those sheets. She drifted off to sleep thinking about how nice it felt to float away on a smooth cloud of comfort, just her and her sweet baby who couldn't possibly feel like it was locked up in jail. Joshua was just teasing her. She smiled a little deeper. It was nice to have someone want to meet her child. She wondered suddenly if the baby could come tonight. As far as she was concerned, it would be welcome anytime.

Chapter Five

Pink streaks from the rising sun were starting to fan out across the skyline when Joshua walked back through the ranch yard early the next morning. He'd broken the ice on the water trough by the corral and fed the horses their grain. The rest of the chores could wait until after breakfast. He ducked his head farther down into the collar of his sheepskin coat and tucked his gloved hands into his pockets. The air was bitter cold, even though the snow had stopped falling sometime late yesterday.

He glanced to the house and didn't see any lights on there yet, but just then he heard a high-pitched girlish squeal coming from the bunkhouse. Rosie must be up and doing something.

He started walking faster. No one ever locked the bunkhouse door, and he hadn't thought to do that this morning, but he should have. Rosie probably thought Mark was there; usually they would both be up by now. Joshua didn't know how Tommy would take to Rosie— or she to him. The squeal didn't sound like a battle cry, but Joshua wasn't sure. Then he remembered the dogs.

He ran the last few yards, and his boots pounded up the steps to the building.

He had scarcely opened the bunkhouse door and stepped inside when he heard the high squeal again. The blast of heat from the stove made his face sting slightly as his skin adjusted to the warmth. He turned to close the door behind him and took his Stetson off so he could see more clearly. No one had turned the lights on yet, and there were a lot of shadows. He wasn't sure Rosie knew where the switch was, and Tommy wouldn't have thought of it.

His eyes went first to the spot where Tommy's dog had slept last night, and he was pleased to see the dog was still lying there, awake but seemingly indifferent to the day. There was no other dog around.

Then he saw five-year-old Rosie standing in a long white flannel nightgown, looking directly at him with her eyes sparkling in excitement.

"I kissed the Sleeping Beauty," Rosie announced in a loud whisper and screeched again, looking delighted as she twirled around in the middle of the bunkhouse floor in her stocking feet. "And she woke up—just like in the fairy tale. Sleeping Beauty woke up. And it was me that did it!"

Rosie's curly red hair bounced, and her pink cheeks shone. Anyone would think she was a cherub in a heavenly choir instead of a night stalker searching for a victim who she could kiss in their sleep. Joshua looked over and noticed the pile of clothing beside the door that consisted of Rosie's puffy winter coat, mittens and snow boots. At least she'd had sense enough to put on her coat before running over here in her nightgown.

Then Joshua scanned the rest of the room. The door

was open to Emma's suite just like it had been last night. Max had his covers pulled over his head and his back to everyone. He appeared to be trying to squeeze a little more sleep out of the night. Joshua doubted Rosie had even tried to kiss the old man. The bird's cage was sitting on a chair near Max's bed and was still hidden by its canvas cover, although some muffled snorts were coming from within so the bird must be awake. Tommy was perched on the edge of his bed in his pajamas, wide-eyed and ready to move. His hair was standing up in every direction, and he seemed captivated by Rosie.

"Did Sleeping Beauty say anything?" Joshua brought his attention back to Rosie and cautiously asked her as he studied the doorway between the two rooms.

Rosie stopped twirling and frowned. "She asked me if I had any coffee." Rosie looked puzzled and asked Joshua. "Do princesses drink coffee?"

"Some of them might," Joshua replied. "Although, this one should drink tea. Does your mother know you're out here?"

"Mama's asleep," Rosie said and put her finger to her lips in the universal signal to be silent. "I have to be quiet all of the time now. That's why I came to see Markie. Mama and the baby are always asleep."

Rosie stood still for a moment as though thinking. "Babies aren't much fun, are they?" She looked at Joshua mournfully. "I thought the baby would be like a puppy, but it's not. It doesn't even wiggle around. I can't pet it. It just lies there like a doll. I don't much like dolls anymore. Do you think it bites?"

"It doesn't have any teeth yet," Joshua said, "so no,

it can't bite. And you can't bite it," he added since this was Rosie, and she liked to experiment.

"Oh," Rosie said, sounding disappointed.

"A baby has a lot of growing to do," Joshua tried to explain. "In a few years, she will be fun to play with."

"Will she know how to play the piano?" Rosie asked, looking hopeful. "Then she could play for me to tap dance."

"Not right away," Joshua said. "Maybe in ten years or so if she has lessons, then she can play."

That did not cheer Rosie up. "Do I have to be quiet that long?"

"Oh, I'm sure things will ease up," Joshua said, deciding he should change the subject and let Mark deal with the child's disappointment. After all, Mark was the one who was going to be her father. He had been in the military for years, and Joshua was beginning to think that might just about be enough training to handle Rosie, especially since Mark had specialized in explosives.

Rosie beckoned for Joshua to bend down, and she put her face close to him when he did. He could hear footsteps in the doorway behind him, but by then Rosie had her hands on his cheeks and wasn't likely to let go.

"I think that princess is going to have a baby, too," she whispered solemnly in Joshua's ear. "Will it be a sleeping baby, too?"

There was nothing soft about Rosie's whisper, and Joshua knew who was standing behind him.

"I think all babies sleep a lot," Joshua said diplomatically as he straightened to his full height.

"It's freezing outside," Emma's voice came from behind, and he turned. She'd obviously slept in her sweatshirt and jeans. He'd have to see about getting some clothes for her, too.

"How's it going?" Joshua asked. "And what are you doing walking around? Doesn't your ankle still hurt?"

"It's fine today," she said and then started to frown. "But what time is it? What are any of us doing up? It's cold."

Joshua smiled. "I'm doing chores. And it would be a lot colder in here if Bailey hadn't put in this new propane-heating system recently. We used to have to get up and shove some wood into the stove every few hours on a night like this. Sometimes we used to go do chores earlier than we needed just to get out of feeding the fire."

Joshua winced. He'd sounded like a grandfather bragging about how far he'd needed to walk to school in the old days.

"I know," Emma said as she yawned and stretched. "That's what I had to do in the trailer. I hated it."

"Well, see, we have all the comforts here," Joshua replied a little stiffly. He couldn't help but stare at Emma, fresh from her sleep. Everything about her was calm and, well…radiant. His eyes even saw a shimmering glow around her head—at least, he thought so. It was hard to be sure with all the shadows. Still, her cheeks were seashell pink; her chestnut hair sparkled as it curled. And her lips—ah, they looked rosy and soft. He knew his tongue would slip up if he tried to tell her any of this so he stayed silent.

"I still want coffee," she said in a disgruntled voice that erased some of the stardust in his fantasy. Her eyes grew sharper until the simmer was all gone.

He couldn't help but sigh. "Ah, well."

"And don't try to talk me into drinking some herbal tea that's been in a jar for a week," she continued. "I might as well drink water out of an irrigation ditch."

"But the baby—" Joshua felt obliged to protest.

"I only take a few tiny sips of coffee," Emma said and then smiled at Rosie. Joshua noticed that the girl brought back some of Emma's glow.

She continued talking to the girl. "I need those little sips as much as I need you, to wake me up completely."

Rosie beamed. "I woke you with my kiss. I did it like in the fairy tale."

"You sure did, sweetheart," Emma said.

Just then Rosie's face crumpled, right before everyone's eyes. "Nobody calls me sweetheart anymore. Nobody talks to me." She looked up at Emma and added tearfully. "Nobody likes me anymore. Not even Mrs. Hargrove. They only like that baby! And it's useless. It can't even bite anything."

With that, Rosie launched herself toward Emma whose arms seemed to automatically open wide to catch the bundle of grief.

"There, there," Emma patted the sobbing girl on the back. Then Emma looked up at Joshua and demanded to know, "What kind of people are these? Can't they see poor Rosie needs some attention, too? And who's Mrs. Hargrove?"

Even Tommy padded over in his stocking feet and patted Rosie on the shoulder. His face puckered up as though he were going to join Rosie in her tears.

"I..." Joshua started to talk but had to clear his throat. "I..." He tried again and couldn't think of an easygoing word to say to take the accusation out of Emma's eyes. Where was his glib tongue when he needed it? "Good people," he finally muttered. "Love her for sure. Mrs. Hargrove is her Sunday school teacher. A good woman."

Emma didn't say anything to him; she just scorched him with her eyes. Then she bent down, as best she could, and kissed Rosie on the top of her head.

Rosie stopped crying and looked up at Emma in awe. Then she turned her gaze to Tommy.

"Was that a princess kiss?" Rosie asked him in a whisper.

"Princess kiss for Rosie," Tommy confirmed in the most emphatic sentence Joshua had ever heard come out of the boy's mouth. Then Tommy smiled at Rosie and kissed her cheek himself before shyly saying "Two kisses for Rosie."

The boy might only be seven years old, but Joshua figured Tommy had found some of the smooth-talking patter that Joshua had lost.

"Well, I'll be," Max muttered from across the room.

With that, Emma swept Rosie and Tommy back into her suite and closed the door. The click of the lock turning sounded like a gunshot, reverberating throughout the room.

"I'll be," Max repeated his words, sounding more astonished than before. "I think Tommy's in love. He usually takes a long time to warm up to strangers."

That door locking didn't seem to bother Max.

Joshua turned to the older man and tried to make light of it. "Who can resist a damsel in distress?"

Max grunted and gave Joshua a meaningful look. "No one here, that's for sure."

Joshua snorted. "That's what you know."

"No need to be touchy about it," the older man said with a yawn. "It happens to us all—time to time."

Joshua walked over and picked up his Stetson from the bench by the door. He went over to the thermostat that regulated the propane stove and made sure it was set to a good temperature, since everyone here was in their pajamas. He stopped to look out the frost-lined window facing the main house and saw there was a light on in the kitchen.

"I'll be back," he said then as he put his hat on his head and turned up the collar of his coat.

"Going to get Emma that coffee, I expect," Max said with a shrug.

"I—" Joshua started to deny it, but he kept walking to the door.

"Get me a cup, too," Max called out. "My joints are bothering me this morning or I'd walk over myself."

There seemed to be no answer to that so Joshua just opened the door and stepped out into the freezing weather. He closed the door firmly behind him. His joints were bothering him, too. And every other part of his body. He decided it must be fifteen degrees below zero. It was early spring, but the weather seemed stuck in winter. He stepped over to the house as fast as he could without slipping on the icy ground.

Usually, the front door of the Rosen house was locked, but he could see it was unlatched this morning, likely thanks to Rosie's escape. Joshua knocked softly, and when he heard Mark's footsteps, Joshua pushed the door open and stepped inside.

"I don't want to wake anyone," he said quietly to Mark, "but we could use some coffee. And some tea. And do you have any juice for the kids?"

"You having a party out there in the bunkhouse?" Mark asked as he turned toward the kitchen. Joshua thought the dark-haired man looked like a lumberjack in his flannel shirt and jeans—which seemed about right, given how the day was shaping up to be. Joshua slipped his boots off and followed him.

"I don't know what it is," Joshua confessed as they crossed the corner of the living room. "All I know is I'm the wicked villain in a fairy tale of Rosie's making. I'll probably get banished from the kingdom when I get back—or bitten, maybe even beheaded."

"Rosie?" Mark stopped inside the kitchen and turned around. "What's she got to do with anything? She's still sleeping in her bed with Mrs. Hargrove."

"That's what you think?" Joshua said with a snort. "You're going to have to up your game, my friend, to keep up with our Rosie."

"She promised me I'd have it easy being her father," Mark said, a twinkle in his eyes. "It didn't even last for seventy-two hours."

"Don't worry," Joshua said. "I have it on good authority that it's been a lifetime for her. She can only be good and quiet for so long."

Mark chuckled. "I figured as much. Do you want some toast to go with your coffee, tea and juice?"

"I'll get to making that." Joshua stepped over to the counter. "And maybe a few bananas would go well, too. How much bread do we have?"

Mark looked up from where he was filling a thermos with coffee. "How many people you got out there, anyway?"

Joshua held his breath for a minute. Technically it wasn't his bunkhouse. "Just Emma Smitt. Her seven-year-old brother, Tommy. And her defender, an old guy named Max."

"Wow," Mark said. He looked surprised.

Joshua took a deep breath. "And Tommy's dog and Max's talking bird, Cupid."

"Cupid?" Mark smiled. "And he talks?"

"Don't kiss the bird," Joshua cautioned. "Believe me, he'll ask you to—"

Mark threw back his head and laughed.

"Maybe I should help you carry breakfast out to the bunkhouse," Mark said then. "This I have to see."

"Oh," Joshua said as he slipped four slices of bread into the toaster. "Spend a few minutes fussing over Rosie while you're there."

Mark turned to him and cocked an eyebrow.

"She's feeling a little displaced by the baby," Joshua said and paused a minute. "And somewhat disappointed in the baby, too. I think she would have rather gotten a puppy."

"She already has a dog," Mark pointed out as he started filling another thermos with hot water.

"Tell her," Joshua said. "Not me."

Joshua decided to bring a jar of Bailey's homemade strawberry jam, too. Emma could use a little sweetening, especially if she didn't get as much coffee as she wanted. He'd located a whole basket full of tea bags of different kinds. At the last minute, he picked up a jar of honey, too.

Joshua had so much to carry that, in the end, he loaded up Rosie's little wagon and pulled it across the yard. Mark was walking beside him, humming away like he was on some great adventure.

"So, Emma Smitt came back with you," Mark said

when they were halfway across the yard. "That's promising."

Joshua stopped, even though they were both freezing their noses off. "I wouldn't make too much of it. She didn't come voluntarily."

"You didn't kidnap her?" Mark asked, looking worried. "I know you're a little sweet on her, but—"

"It was circumstances, that's all," Joshua said. "And I'm not sweet on anybody. I was her last choice for help, but I was also her only choice. I'm still not sure she'll stay."

"Well, you'll charm her if you have a few days," Mark said as he started walking again.

"I wouldn't count on that," Joshua muttered as he began pulling the wagon again. He'd never admitted to Mark, or anyone else, that he'd lost all his smooth-talking ways. It wasn't something a guy could exactly ask the church prayer group to take up on his behalf. No, he'd have to suffer in silence without his glib tongue. It would have been better if he'd sprained his ankle when he gave up gambling. That he could at least get fixed.

He let Mark lead the way to the bunkhouse. Joshua wasn't totally sure how this day was going to turn out. Although, he did need to go to Miles City and look for shoes and some other clothes for Tommy. Emma should have some new clothes, too, and she should see a doctor. Maybe if he kept everyone busy in Miles City, they would forget they wanted to leave here as soon as they could.

Emma was settled back on the bed listening to Rosie tell about the talent show that she'd won. The timeline wasn't quite clear as to when she'd done that. But the girl even got up and tried to tap dance in her stocking feet so she could show them how she'd triumphed, snatching the prize away from some Baker boy—which apparently was a big coup, although Rosie never explained why the boy was important. Finally, Rosie fell to the floor in exhaustion, or perhaps she was trying a ballet move as a swan. It didn't matter. Emma, and even Tommy, applauded enthusiastically when Rosie stood and took a final bow.

Rosie let them clap for a few moments.

"It's better with my tap shoes and my cane," Rosie explained anxiously. "I don't have a real top hat, but I can use a cowboy one."

"I think it was lovely just the way it was," Emma assured her firmly, even though she had stopped applauding by then. For the first time since Joshua had shown up on her mountain, she thought she might be able to stay here on the ranch until the baby was born. Everything looked brighter now that she had a friend here, even if that friend was only five years old.

"Rosie dance," Tommy added with a nod of his head. "Rosie good dance."

Emma figured Tommy had a friend, too.

Rosie climbed back on top of the bed with them. The satin-squared quilt was crumpled but warm. Emma knew they needed to get dressed, but she was wearing the only clothes she had with her, and she didn't know if Tommy would like to wear that pumpkin costume any longer. He couldn't stay in his pajamas all day, though.

By then Emma looked up and noticed that Max was standing in the open doorway.

"What did I miss?" the older man asked with a slow smile on his face. "Sounded exciting in here."

"I danced," Rosie said as she spread her arms wide. "Like the wind."

"That's right," Emma said. "Rosie was showing us her dance moves. You and Cupid would have both enjoyed it."

"Cupid?" Rosie asked as she turned to Max. "Like the Valentine baby?"

"Cupid's not a baby," Emma said without thinking.

"Is too," Rosie replied indignantly. "Only babies wear diapers, and that Cupid wears one. That's why he makes people get married. All babies need a mommy and a daddy, even him—that's why Cupid shoots them with his arrow. Boing!" She demonstrated the arrow hitting its target. "Then the people get wounded, and when they're down they fall in love." Rosie stopped and frowned. "Does he hurt them with his arrows? Are they going to bleed to death if they don't fall in love? That's not very nice of Cupid."

"Hush. Don't say his name," Max urged them quietly. "He's starting to—"

There was no need to say more because they could all hear the slowly rising shriek coming from the other part of the bunkhouse. At that moment, the door to the outside opened. Emma could feel the rush of cold air coming into her room, even though she could not see who had entered. Of course, it wasn't a secret. It had to be Joshua. She could almost smell the coffee. Before she could even call out and ask him what he brought back, the screech in the other room exploded.

"Kiss the bird," the call came louder than Emma would have thought possible. "Kiss the bird."

"I didn't know you had a bird," Rosie turned to Emma and exclaimed in delight as she scooted off the bed and headed for the open doorway.

"It's not my bird," Emma explained, but it was too late. The girl was already gone.

"We better go after her," Max said, a bit of worry in his voice. "Cupid isn't used to children."

"Who's he used to then?" Emma asked as she moved to the edge of the bed and stood up.

"Drunken sailors," Max told her as he nodded toward the outer room. "He's got a vocabulary to match, too. Kiss the bird is mild for him."

"Oh, great," Emma said as she started walking to the doorway. Bailey Rosen would not be happy with her at all, not if she corrupted her sweet little girl with that kind of talk.

By the time Emma got through the door, Joshua and another man about his age were standing on a large faded rug. Their arms were filled with metal thermoses and plastic bags full of what looked like toast.

"That's some bird," the man she didn't know said with a nod toward Cupid.

"Oh, dear," Emma said, rushing up to hold Rosie back a little. The girl had her nose up to within inches of Cupid's cage. She was far enough away since the cage was sitting on that wooden chair, but she was straining to get closer. Rosie did her best to study the bird, and Cupid was eyeing the girl right back. He didn't look friendly.

"Kiss the bird," Cupid demanded again, ruffling his feathers and sounding upset. He took a step closer to the bars where Rosie stood. Emma pulled the girl back an inch.

"I can't kiss you," Rosie answered the parrot in frustration. "You don't have any lips. How can anyone kiss you?"

Rosie turned from the bird in distress and addressed Joshua and the other man. "How can I kiss him? He's just got that old beak. He shouldn't ask me to do something like that."

"I don't think he really means for you to kiss him," Joshua said gently as he set the bags he was carrying down on the small table in the corner. "It's just Cupid's way of getting attention."

Joshua then took off his hat and set it on the table. Emma noticed his eyes were kind, and he seemed fond of Rosie as he knelt down to her level.

"Well, I would never do something like that," Rosie said, lifting her chin and looking self-righteous. "Mama always says good girls get all the attention they need by being good. Bad girls get a time-out."

Emma doubted Rosie lived by that maxim, but it was an interesting one.

She looked over in time to see Joshua stand up and wave to encompass the entire room. "Everyone, this is Mark Dakota." He nodded his head toward the other man. "Mark, this is Emma Smitt, Tommy Smitt, and Max, who is the owner of Cupid."

"Markie's going to be my new daddy," Rosie added proudly.

Emma met Mark's eyes and nodded. Once she got a good look at him, she recognized Mark from the meeting with the attorney. She didn't think, at the time, that Bailey Rosen was involved with anyone. But things had obviously changed. The woman had exhibited no loyalty to Junior at all. Emma knew better than anyone else that Junior had not been faithful to Bailey, but it couldn't be right to move on with her life so fast after he'd died.

Emma realized everyone was still talking about the bird while she was thinking disgruntled thoughts, and she brought her attention back to what was happening.

"I wouldn't rightly say I own that bird," Max was correcting Joshua's introduction. "I feed him, and he keeps me company. His heart has always belonged to my Navy buddy, though."

"So is the buddy going to come back and get him?" Joshua asked. Emma was wondering the same thing. She had never heard this part of the story.

Max shook his head. "My buddy died some years ago. He used to kiss Cupid all the time. Best of friends, they were. Taught him to ask for kisses, too."

Emma saw the scowl slip away from Rosie's face, and a look of pure sweetness come over it. "Oh, the poor birdie. He must feel like I did when my daddy died—" She stopped and swallowed. Then she looked over at Mark with a trace of guilt in her eyes. "My first daddy. Not my new daddy."

Emma was slammed with her own wave of grief. The girl was sorry about Junior. Ever since Emma had found out about Junior's death, it had seemed that she was the only one on the planet that felt any loss at his passing. But now there was this small child who mourned him, too.

She leaned closer to Rosie and wrapped her in her arms again. It felt good just to hold her.

"I'm sorry about your first daddy," Emma whispered as she patted Rosie on the back. She was surprised when Rosie's little hand patted her back, too.

Everyone was silent for a few minutes.

Finally, Joshua spoke. "One thing I'll say for Junior. He would have wanted both of you to have good lives. He always was in favor of a good time."

Emma felt a tear slip down her face at that, but she had to smile. That was one thing everyone could say for Junior. He believed in enjoying life. It wasn't much of a legacy, but it was something.

Joshua cleared his throat after another minute. "We've got coffee and tea just waiting to be had. And the toast is getting cold, so we should eat it while we can."

Mark had already started to open up the bags they had brought. Joshua went into Emma's suite and brought back some mugs from the cupboard there.

"You won't have to bring food over again," Emma said as they all got a cup of hot beverage. "When I get a chance to buy some groceries, I can cook here."

Mark looked up in astonishment. He'd taken a seat on one of the bunks and had been cradling his coffee cup in his hands. "You aren't going to eat with us in the main house?" he asked. "Everyone does. I just assumed you—"

"I don't want to be a bother to Bailey," Emma said, sounding every bit as self-righteous as Rosie had earlier. "She just had a baby and—"

"Oh, Bailey won't be doing the cooking," Mark said. "That will be Joshua and me doing the honors."

"Yes." Rosie nodded and added solemnly as though she had been coached, "And we're grateful for any food that is put on our plates, no matter who cooked it or even if it's burned or even if it's liver." The girl shuddered. "Or cauliflower. Or stewed tomatoes. Or—"

"We get the message, Rosie," Joshua said with a grimace in Emma's direction. "We do the cooking, but we're open to help if you're of a mind to give it. We'd help, of course. And Rosie always sets the table."

"Oh," Emma said, turning everything around in her mind. This made a big difference. She'd be giving, not receiving. "I make an excellent lasagna. And Swedish meatballs. Beef stew and biscuits. And a few other dishes you might like."

"Can you make chocolate pudding?" Rosie whispered with hope clear in her voice as she drew back from Emma's arms. "Markie and Joshua can't make it right. It has little lumps in it."

"Lumps in their pudding?" Emma looked over to see both Joshua and Mark hanging their heads.

"We follow the directions on the box," Joshua said defensively.

"Mostly," Mark added. "We don't know what goes wrong."

Emma stood up and smoothed down her sweatshirt. "Let me know what you have in the way of supplies, and I'll make something for supper. Lunch, too, I guess."

"Not lunch," Joshua said. "You and Tommy are coming with me to Miles City. Max, too, if he wants. We'll get something to eat there. But I have a doctor's appointment for you, Emma, and Tommy and I need to get him some shoes and a few other things."

"Come say hello to Bailey before you leave," Mark addressed the invitation to Emma. "She'll be awake before you go, and she'll want to meet you again."

Emma frantically tried to think of an excuse not

to do any such thing when Rosie put her hand inside Emma's.

"You have to meet my mommy," Rosie assured her. "You're the only friend I have who I woke with a princess kiss."

Emma looked over at Joshua for rescue. He was no help. "It'll only take a minute. We'll take Tommy, too," he said.

Emma touched her earlobes.

"I'll need my earrings," she mumbled.

"I got the one right here," Joshua said as he tapped his shirt pocket.

Emma nodded. If she was going to meet one of those well-dressed charity women, she needed to wear her diamond earrings. She would never tell Bailey where she'd gotten those earrings, but the message they sent was that someone had thought Emma Smitt was worth wearing diamonds. Glittering, expensive diamonds, she told herself, like the ones they had in high-class magazine ads. She could meet anyone if she had those diamonds in her ears.

She rubbed her earlobes again. She hoped it wasn't showing off to wear those earrings. She vividly remembered when Junior had given them to her. She'd felt special. If she found a jewelry store, she might even have the silver spheres on them cleaned. They were her most priceless possession, and she needed to take care of them.

She felt her baby kick and put her hands on her stomach. The earrings weren't her only reminder of Junior. She wondered how she was ever going to provide a good life for her coming child.

Chapter Six

Joshua felt the sun on his head. The day had started unseasonably cold, but it was warming until it must be thirty-some degrees outside. It was finally spring. He'd finished his chores over an hour ago. That meant Emma and Tommy had been inside the main house for all that time talking to Bailey. That didn't bode well. He knew Emma had a bit of a temper at times. And Tommy could be unpredictable, as well. What could be keeping them? He had expected Mark to take them inside the house, introduce them, let everyone chit-chat for a few minutes and then lead them back to the bunkhouse.

Joshua had already taken the dog food and Emma's suitcase out of the back of his pickup and carried them into the bunkhouse. He had even changed into a white shirt and was now holding his going-to-church Stetson in his hands. Everything was ready, he thought, as he stood by his open pickup door and fretted about what could have gone wrong.

It occurred to him that he was hovering like an old mother hen, but he couldn't seem to help it.

"Bailey wouldn't object to Tommy," Joshua muttered, ticking off his worries. "And surely Emma won't tell Bailey that if she had been a better wife Junior wouldn't have gone looking elsewhere." Joshua paused. The worries could add up on a man. He should have insisted on going with Emma and her brother when Mark took them in to meet Bailey.

Joshua was almost going to go to the house and check on what was happening when he saw the front door open. Emma stepped out wearing her coat open and a pretty sparkling blue top showing beneath it. Tommy had on a red sweatshirt that Joshua had never seen before. The boy also had on his stepfather's old coat. Rosie was standing at the open door waving them off.

"Ready to go?" he asked when Emma and Tommy got close enough to hear him.

Emma nodded. Tommy looked up and grinned at him.

"Okay." Joshua tried to keep the worry out of his voice as he lifted his black Stetson from behind his leg and put it on his head, pushing it down slightly so it would stay there in any wind that might come along.

The startled gasp from Tommy halted everything. Joshua looked down and saw the boy frantically trying to hide behind Emma. His eyes were again filled with fear, and he looked almost sick.

"What?" Joshua said almost involuntarily. What had happened?

Not knowing what else to do, Joshua reached up and took his Stetson off his head. He held the hat at his side as he watched Tommy's trembling stop. The boy gave him a slight smile. Joshua looked down at his hat, careful to not raise it to where Tommy could see it.

"It's my hat," Joshua said to Emma. "Tommy's afraid of my hat?"

Emma had bent down to put her arm around Tommy and she looked up, her eyes filled with confusion. "Why would he be afraid of a hat?"

"I don't know," Joshua said in a low voice as he took a step closer to them both. "Maybe he was afraid of someone who wore a hat like this."

"Our stepfather," Emma said with sudden confidence in her voice. "That must be it. He always wore a Stetson. Part of being a rodeo rider, he said. He wore it to show off."

"Well, I wear mine to keep the sun out of my eyes and off my neck when I'm working," Joshua said. "No need to show off to the cows."

"How about it, Tommy?" Joshua said as he squatted down to be closer to the boy. "Do you like my hat?" Joshua lifted his hat up so the boy could see it.

Tommy shook his head vigorously, looking down and then squeezing himself behind Emma again.

"Well, that's my answer," Joshua said as he stood up, relieved that it was a simple reason and not him that scared Tommy.

"But wouldn't Tommy see that it was you and not my stepfather wearing it?" Emma asked.

Joshua thought that was a good question. He studied Tommy a minute and then pointed back at the house. "Tommy, how many balls are in the box by the porch?"

Joshua watched as Tommy squinted and tried to focus his eyes on the location where Joshua pointed.

"Has he ever had his eyes checked?" Joshua asked Emma.

"Oh, I'm sure my stepfather would know to do that,"

she said and then hesitated. "But really I don't know. Maybe he thought the schools would do it, or maybe he just didn't think about it."

Joshua nodded. "There's an eye doctor in the same clinic building as where you have your appointment. They might be able to slip him in for a quick session just to see what shape his eyes are in."

Joshua could see Emma trying to think of a way to say no.

"I don't have—" she started to say and then stopped, letting her voice trail off. She sounded defeated. She led Tommy to the pickup.

"If it's the money," Joshua assured her as he watched them approach the passenger side, "I can cover it."

"No," she said, shaking her head as she stood outside the door he'd already opened for them. "I don't want to start borrowing from people when I don't know how I'll pay them back. It's bad enough that you're taking me to see a baby doctor, but that's something I suppose I need to do. Tommy's eyes can wait a week or two until I can figure out how to get a job."

Joshua didn't want to discourage Emma, but he thought she'd have her hands full with a new baby without looking for a job.

"It's only money," Joshua protested. "You don't have to pay it back."

"Then, it is charity," Emma said crisply. "And you know how I feel about that."

"Let me check with the eye doctor," Joshua said. "I think Montana has a program for kids that go to school. There might not be any charge. I'm assuming he does need to go to school?"

"Oh, yes," Emma said. "I haven't figured out how or where, but he'll have to have school."

"Maybe the doctor will know about that, too," Joshua said.

"But we'll be in the mountains," Emma protested. "I mean after the baby comes."

Joshua arched his eyebrow. "Where would he go to school there?"

"I have to figure that out," Emma said as she neared the vehicle, clearly exasperated. "I don't know yet."

Joshua kept pace with her. She was one stubborn woman and she'd figure something out. Or she'd have to resign herself to living here. He did wish he could talk her into doing just that, but his tongue was clumsy, and he was likely to make it worse.

Joshua walked closer to lift Tommy into the seat and was going to help Emma up when she stopped.

"Oh, I'm not thinking," she said as she turned slightly and faced Joshua. "I'll need to get that letter from my stepfather showing that I have guardianship of Tommy. The eye doctor would probably need that if there's a government program."

"That might help," Joshua said as she turned to step back into the bunkhouse. Joshua was not sure if that paper would work for the government, but maybe the doctor would accept it.

Emma came back from the bunkhouse waving the envelope.

"Got it," she said as she made her way back to the open door. Joshua helped lift her a little so she could slip into the seat beside Tommy.

Joshua walked around to the driver's side and

stepped in. Once seated, he carefully placed his Stetson on the dash of his cab.

Joshua started the pickup and drove down the lane. They were barely out on the gravel road before he looked over and commented, "You're both dressed up and looking fine."

Tommy patted the sweatshirt where it covered his stomach. "Red nice."

Emma grimaced. "Bailey insisted I take this top. She said it was one of her old maternity ones, and she said that she certainly didn't need it now and that I could use it until the baby comes. I'm not keeping it so it's borrowing and not the other. But it's much too fancy for wearing around."

Emma sounded particularly joyless about the top as she continued. "She said it matched my earrings."

"She's right about that," Joshua commented. Swirls of deep blue curved over white in a pretty pattern with a row of rhinestones that circled the neckline. The stones sparkled like the earrings. And the whole thing kind of billowed. It made Emma look delicate and sophisticated at the same time.

"I told her my earrings were diamonds," Emma confessed. "I hope it didn't make her feel bad. I'm not sure she has such nice earrings. I wasn't going to say anything, but I did."

"I know how that can happen," Joshua said. "Happens to me sometimes when I'm nervous."

"It's not that," Emma said.

"What is it, then?" Joshua asked.

The miles were passing, and Tommy had fallen asleep at Emma's side.

"Bailey told me the blouse would work for when I

go to church," Emma added finally and turned slightly toward him. "Church! I don't go to church. That's when I mentioned my diamonds. To show her I was somebody—sort of, you know, even if I don't go to church."

"People who wear diamonds go to church, too," Joshua said when nothing more seemed to be coming on the topic. "Did you mention that you don't usually go?"

"How could I?" Emma asked and closed her eyes. "Rosie was there looking at me like I really am her very own private princess. I think the diamonds have her fooled. But how could I admit I don't go to church? What kind of a princess doesn't go to church?"

They were both silent for a few minutes. Joshua had never even considered that question before.

"Well, Rosie will find out on Sunday that you're not there," Joshua finally pointed out. He hadn't expected to care so much about Emma's feelings, but he did.

"No, Rosie won't be disappointed," Emma said and groaned. She opened her eyes and looked over at him in despair. "I'm going to be there, wearing my earrings. I promised."

Joshua grinned and then got serious. "So do you not go to church because you hate the thought, or is it simple indifference?"

"My mother used to take me when I was little," Emma said. "Before my real father died. Back then, I remember believing. I was so earnest I even prayed every night before I went to sleep. But then, after my mother married my stepfather, everything changed. I didn't think God cared much about me. No one went to church in my stepfather's house; he saw to that. And my mother never mentioned God when my stepfather was around. That man owned her. I used to wish we could go to church again together, but we never did."

"Well, Sunday you can go in her honor, then."

They were both silent for a minute, and then Emma asked softly, "Do you think God loves us? Like my mother used to say."

Joshua smiled. "Yes, I do. It took me a while to figure it out, but I do believe He loves each of us. Yes, I do."

Joshua was willing to accept that God wanted what was best for him so he believed in God's love. He still wasn't sure that God really had his back, though—not in the hard times. After all, his father had likely felt some love for him and his sister, but it hadn't meant he could be trusted to do what needed to be done for their care. A person couldn't be trusted if they didn't even pay attention to what was happening to the other person.

"I don't think those church people will like me going to their church," Emma admitted after some silence. "I'm not married, and I'm having a baby."

"Nobody said you need to be perfect to go to church," Joshua said. "It's the opposite, in fact. We all make mistakes."

Emma sighed. "Well, I guess I'll see."

"It'll be okay," Joshua said. He told himself he'd make sure no one said anything unkind. Not that it was likely, anyway.

"Bailey even talked me into some kind of Bible study that Mrs. Hargrove leads for mothers," Emma admitted after a little more time had passed. "They're going to meet the day after tomorrow at Bailey's house. A Mrs. Baker is going to come. Rosie said the woman needs to be a very careful mother because she has the Baker boys to make behave. I've never heard of a mother needing to be careful before."

Joshua chuckled. "Rosie doesn't think much of those Baker boys. At least, she won't admit to thinking much of them. She doesn't like that they don't do what she says."

The longer Joshua sat with the knowledge that Emma was going to church, the more he wanted to grin. He wasn't sure Emma would like that, though, so he tried keeping the grin inside. That didn't work so he started to whistle.

"What's got you so happy?" Emma looked over at him with a half smile on her face. "Only women get to go to the Bible study, and Rosie tells me there will be cookies."

Joshua winced at that. "Did she say which cookies?"

"Oatmeal raisin," Emma answered.

"I was afraid of that," Joshua muttered.

"Cookies for Tommy?" the boy asked. Joshua didn't know when Emma's brother had woken up. He was all boy, though, and not about to lose a chance at a sweet.

"I'm not sure you'll want these cookies," Joshua answered. "We, uh… Mark and I, we didn't exactly get the measurements right."

Emma shrugged. "Don't worry. Lots of cooks make little adjustments to their recipes. Likely no one will be able to tell."

"We got the tablespoons and the teaspoons confused," Joshua confessed. "Big measuring spoon. Little measuring spoon."

"Oh," Emma grimaced. "That might make a difference."

"That's why it's important to be able to see," Joshua said as he glanced down at Tommy. "Some things you need to see to get straight. Otherwise your cookies can be too salty to eat."

"No cookies?" Tommy asked Joshua in concern.

"Don't worry," Joshua answered. "I'll buy some at the store."

"Store," Tommy repeated with a nod. He looked relieved.

Joshua kept whistling as he drove. Emma and Tommy were coming to church on Sunday. And she wanted to know more about God.

"Please, Lord, make yourself known to Emma and Tommy," Joshua prayed silently. He had a feeling that they had ears ready to listen. A Sunday service and one of Mrs. Hargrove's Bible studies would grab Emma's interest. Joshua would see if Rosie would share some of her children's Bible books with Tommy.

Joshua hadn't been a Christian for long, but it made a big difference in his life. He wasn't sure what possibilities it would open up for Emma, but she needed to know God loved her.

He glanced over at Emma, feeling suddenly panicked that she might be able to read his mind. Not many people wanted to be prayed over if they weren't already Christians. She didn't seem to be paying any attention to him, though. And then he saw she'd brought out that handkerchief she twisted when she was worried. He wondered what was wrong now.

The day was growing warmer, Emma thought as she sat there twisting her handkerchief in the shadow of Tommy's shoulders. She missed her mother. Joshua had stopped talking, and it was just as well there was silence. A steady drizzle of water slid down the windshield of the pickup. She knew that meant the layer of snow that was on top of the vehicle when they had left the ranch was melting. The streets in Miles City had no ice on them. Even the dirty drifts along the sides of the road were turning to slush. But all she wanted was for Joshua to turn the pickup around and go home.

Emma dreaded facing a doctor and needing to confess that she hadn't done anything right in her pregnancy. At the beginning, she'd taken some vitamins, but she'd used the last of them a month ago. She knew her baby was alive because she had felt it kick for a long time now. But all of that breathing stuff that Joshua had talked about—she hadn't done any of that. And she deserved to be scolded.

She was tense by the time Joshua drove the pickup into an area with a brick building that had a big *Medical Clinic* sign in front. Emma looked around at all of the little signs on the post, too. There had to be a dozen different doctors in this location. She smiled when she noticed there was also a jewelry store at one end, as well. The staff there would likely have some of those small cloths that would shine up the silver on her earrings.

"Your appointment is in ten minutes," Joshua said. "Tommy and I could go in with you and get you signed in. There's quite a bit of paperwork since you're a first-time patient. Then I can take Tommy over to the eye doctor if you want, or we can wait for you."

Emma noticed Joshua seemed to make it a point to not look at her directly. She wondered if he thought she would cause trouble. Or maybe he was embarrassed to be taking a pregnant woman to the doctor's appointment, like maybe people would think Joshua was the baby's father.

"I have nothing against seeing a doctor," she said half-truthfully as she slipped her handkerchief back into her pocket. "I just didn't know a doctor to go to before. And I was…maybe I was a little in denial."

Emma glanced over quickly and saw him relax.

He nodded. "It's hard to be in denial of a pregnancy for too long."

"But there's no point in you waiting while I see the doctor," she added as she woke her brother. "Go ahead and take Tommy to the eye doctor. Maybe we'll both finish faster that way. Tell the eye doctor I'll come over when I finish so that I can sign any forms and make payment arrangements if there isn't any program which he qualifies for. Oh, and here's that letter."

Emma pulled the envelope out of her purse and gave it to Joshua. He put it in his shirt pocket and then opened the truck door.

Emma took a deep breath. She'd have to make arrangements to pay for her doctor visit, too. Hopefully, the doctor had a billing program that gave patients thirty days to pay. She reached up and slipped both earrings off. She'd just keep those in her purse. She probably wasn't the only woman with diamonds that was also broke, but she didn't want to advertise these earrings. If she had to pawn them, she would do that to cover the bills. But she'd prefer to wait until the last minute to give them up. She opened her door, and Joshua was there to help her and Tommy down.

Then he walked with her and Tommy into the medical clinic and guided them through a door marked

Obstetrician and to the reception area. Emma noted there were four other pregnant women in the waiting area, each with a man sitting near her who was probably her husband.

Emma stopped at the window, gave her name, and received a clipboard with a form to fill out.

"I'll be fine," Emma whispered to Joshua when the three of them sat down in the plastic chairs. The receptionist said someone would come from the back offices to get her shortly. "Why don't you go to the other office and see about Tommy?"

"You're sure?" he asked.

Emma nodded. "The truth is I can use a few minutes to gather my thoughts. And I have this form to deal with."

It would also spare Joshua from being mistaken for her baby's father, Emma thought. She could see the other men in the room eyeing Joshua as though they might want to ask him to be in a support group with them. She didn't want to impose any further on him. He was a good man. She wondered suddenly why he wasn't already married. Those other men seemed to think he was a possibility. And, when she took a good look at Joshua, she noticed that he was really very attractive. His brown eyes crinkled with warmth; his dark hair had a slight curl to it; his chin was decisive. She'd always liked a strong chin.

The realization that she found him handsome surprised her so much that she blushed.

"You okay?" Joshua asked, his eyes focused on her. "Are you having a hot flash?"

"Pregnant women don't have hot flashes," she whispered low enough so the other men and women in the room wouldn't hear. She didn't want them to think she and Joshua were ignorant. "They have cravings."

Joshua grinned. "Ice cream and pickles. We'll get some of both at the store."

"That would be nice," Emma said, hoping to end the conversation with some dignity. People were starting to look at them.

"Ice cream?" Tommy echoed. "Strawberry?"

Joshua turned to Tommy. "We'll get a few flavors. How about we go get your eyes checked, champ?"

Tommy stood up eagerly. Joshua took her brother's hand, and the two of them walked out of the waiting room. She knew the ophthalmology office was down the hall.

"Just friends," Emma muttered vaguely to the couples that had been watching.

"He's not the baby's father?" the youngest of the women asked softly. She had long blond hair and looked sweet, all round and pink like she was.

"No," Emma said and looked back down at her questionnaire. She still felt people watching her. It made her nervous. She looked up. "I ran out of vitamins, too, and stopped taking them a month ago."

"Ask your doctor," the same woman suggested. "They usually have samples."

"Thank you," Emma said and then smiled politely. "I've got to finish the form."

She got several nods, but no one asked anything else after that.

She spent a few minutes answering the questions on the form. She had to leave some of the answers blank. She didn't have an address that would do them any good. She didn't have insurance. And she didn't have a next-of-kin contact except for Tommy, and she could hardly use him. She did list Junior as the baby's father.

When she took the form back to the receptionist, the woman told her that the doctor was running late, and it would be at least another fifteen minutes before she would be called.

"Do I have time to make a quick trip over to the jewelry store in the building?" Emma asked.

"Sure," the receptionist said. "It's close. Just don't stay too long."

"I won't."

Emma hurried out of the waiting room and down the hall to where the jewelry store was tucked into the side of the building. She wanted to have the silver spheres on her earrings polished. The spheres had a southwestern design on them, and the diamonds hung over the marks and sparkled as she walked. She loved those earrings. Wearing them gave her self-esteem a boost, and she wanted them shining when she met all the people around Dry Creek. She supposed it was shallow, but she had spent so much of her life poorer than anyone else that those earrings helped her feel like she belonged. In high school, she had never had the right clothes or shoes. It had stopped her from making friends. She wished she'd had her earrings back then.

Emma pulled the door open to the jewelry shop and stepped inside. Everything gleamed and shone. The wood floor was polished. The chrome outline of the glass cases reflected the overhead lights. A middle-aged man in a white shirt and black vest was standing behind one of the counters.

"Can I help you?" he asked.

Emma nodded. "I was wondering if you sell those

cloths that people use to shine silver." She reached into her purse and pulled out her earrings. "I wanted to shine these up. They're a bit tarnished, and I want to keep them nice."

"Of course you do," the man said with a smile. "We don't sell those cloths—I know the kind you mean—but I can get rid of that bit of tarnish in a few seconds with the cream I use."

"Oh, that would be so helpful," Emma said as she placed the earrings on the counter. "How much will that be?"

"For that little bit of work?" the man said, "I couldn't charge you anything."

"I should pay something," Emma protested.

The man shook his head. "Just think of me the next time you want some fine jewelry."

"I…well…" Emma hesitated and then decided she was being foolish. She could come back in the future maybe and buy some small thing. "Okay."

The man picked up one of her earrings.

"Some fine scroll work on the silver," he commented as he applied a cream and rubbed it. He did the same to the second earring. And then he took out a microscope of some kind and studied the earrings through it. "Very nice."

"Thank you," Emma murmured, feeling proud. When the man finished, those earrings were as beautiful as when Junior had given them to her. They were her proof that Junior had loved her, no matter what he'd done to fake their wedding.

"I don't think I've ever seen finer cubic zirconia, either," the man continued his praise with a smile on his face.

It took Emma a moment to hear him. "What?"

"The cubic zirconium crystals are exceptional," the man repeated as he put the earrings in a small bag. "They wouldn't fool a jeweler who really looked at them, but most people on the street would take them for diamonds."

Emma was stunned.

"Here you go," the man said as he handed the bag to her. "It's been a pleasure to serve you."

"Thank you," Emma managed to whisper as she took the bag and put it in her purse. She wished she could take the earrings outside and bury them in a deep pit. She was ashamed that she had so readily accepted Junior's word on his gift. She'd thought it was proof of his love, but it was only a measure of how gullible she was. She never should have trusted Junior about anything.

Emma turned and walked out of the shop. That was not the end of her day, either. She had to go to the doctor's appointment. Joshua would ask about that, and she didn't want to tell him what had happened at the jeweler's. She didn't want to lie to him, either. The only thing to do was to carry on like everything was the same as it had been when she saw him and Tommy last.

Emma kept her emotions frozen as she talked with the doctor. The woman was kind, and she didn't scold Emma for not doing what she should have done. Instead, she was reassuring and checked her out fully. Then she gave Emma a sheet with a telephone number to call and an address of where to go when the birth pains signaled that the baby was coming.

"Thank you," Emma said once she had her own clothes back on.

"Here are some multivitamins," the doctor said, giving Emma a large bottle. "And a book for you to read."

"Thank you," Emma repeated, almost in tears by then. She wasn't accustomed to so much kindness. "I'll pay when—"

The doctor interrupted her with a wave of her hand. "We'll talk about that after the delivery. We have so many payment options that you'll find one you can live with. I don't like my new mothers to worry about money."

Emma blinked back her tears and nodded. "Thank you."

"Oh," the doctor said when Emma was almost at the door. "I just saw your intake form. You didn't list a next of kin. Is there a friend or someone else you trust? Someone we could notify in case of an emergency?"

Emma felt the walls pressing in on her. Junior had been the last person she'd trusted, and that hadn't turned out well. She had to say something so she finally said, "In an emergency, you can contact Joshua Spencer at the Rosen Ranch."

"We have contact information for Bailey Rosen," the doctor said. "Would that be the same phone number?"

"Close enough." Emma could barely see for the tears that threatened, but she managed to walk out of the office. She wiped her eyes and saw Joshua and Tommy sitting on a bench by the main door, waiting for her.

She only took a few steps forward before Joshua rushed to her side.

"What's wrong?" he demanded, his tone more worried than she'd ever heard it. A scowl lined his face. "Is something wrong with the baby?"

Without waiting for an answer, Joshua put his arms around her and crushed her to him. She clung to him.

"The baby is fine," she whispered as tears streaked down her face and fell against his coat. She couldn't stop them.

"It's not you, is it? Is something wrong with you?" Joshua asked, sounding even more frantic. His arms gripped her, and she felt safe.

"No," Emma said. "I'm fine. The baby is fine."

"Thank God," Joshua whispered. He didn't release her, though. She stood there in his arms while her breathing settled down.

Finally, Emma confessed, "I gave them your name as an emergency contact. I didn't mean to—I just couldn't think of anyone."

"You did exactly right," Joshua said as he patted her on her back.

They stood like that for a few minutes more until Emma finally realized Tommy was looking at them with alarm in his eyes.

"It's okay." She wiped the tears off her face and smiled at her brother.

Joshua must have also been thinking of Tommy, because he smiled at the boy, too. "Nothing to worry about."

Tommy nodded.

Joshua wasn't releasing her, though, and he put his lips to her ears. "What's wrong? And don't tell me that it's nothing. You don't cry for nothing."

Emma almost started to cry again, but she refused to turn into a watering pot. She drew herself together, and then she felt the soft kiss Joshua placed on her forehead. She couldn't help herself.

"I'm a fake," she wailed as the tears fell again. "My life is a fake."

Joshua reared back to stare at her. "What do you mean?"

"My earrings aren't diamonds," she whispered to him. Her throat was sore, and she had to force herself to continue. Her hand made a fist without her deciding to do so. "Junior told me they were diamonds, but they're not. The jewelry-store man said they are cubic zirconium. Junior must have thought I was a fool the way I was so excited to receive them."

Joshua's face looked pained. "Oh, I'm sorry. I'm sure he didn't think—"

"Don't patronize me," Emma said wearily. Her forehead still felt warm where he'd kissed her. She tried to ignore it, though, and then she felt Tommy's hand anxiously searching for hers. "I just want to go home."

She opened her fist and enclosed her brother's small hand with a squeeze.

"Shoes," Tommy said softly.

"That's right," Emma admitted. She wiped the last tear away. "I forgot."

She looked down and saw that Tommy had brown frame glasses on his round face.

"Don't you look handsome?" she said as she bent down to adjust his glasses slightly. "Can you see better?"

Tommy nodded. "Me see Emma."

She looked up at Joshua. "How bad was his eyesight?"

"Not good," Joshua said with a wink to Tommy. "But the doctor set him up with a pair of loaner glasses that are close to what he needs. We're to come back in a few weeks and order a pair for his prescription."

Emma nodded. She would definitely need to get a job as soon as possible. She had worked as a waitress before, and she didn't know what else she would qualify to do.

Joshua escorted her to his pickup as though she was fine china and in danger of breaking. She knew how most men felt about women who cried on their shoulder so she couldn't blame him for not wanting a repeat of her tears.

"Usually I don't fall apart like that," she said to Joshua as he opened the pickup door and hoisted Tommy up into the seat.

"It's not a problem," Joshua answered. "I want you to tell me your troubles."

Emma figured that statement wasn't worth the effort it took to deny it. No man wanted to hear the worries of a pregnant woman who had no job, no husband and no bank account. She didn't bother saying anything, though.

Instead, she just put her hands on the doorframe as Joshua lifted her up. She had to keep herself together for Tommy and the baby. She would have the baby, and then she'd get a job and pay back every single favor people were doing for her. She'd be fine. If she could just make it through the rest of the day without more tears.

Chapter Seven

Joshua took a deep breath after shutting the passenger door and rubbing his hand over the back of his neck to soothe his tension. Emma and Tommy were safe inside. Emma had stopped crying, and Tommy could finally see.

Joshua felt like he was falling apart, though. He opened his coat as he walked around to the other side of the pickup. He needed to cool down. He'd never been so angry at anyone as he was with Junior. Emma had trusted that man, and look how he'd rewarded her. There was nothing Joshua could do about it though so he opened his door and hauled himself up into the seat. He'd just carry on.

Joshua had barely begun to back out of the parking space when Emma spoke.

"I should have known about Junior," she said softly. She bit her bottom lip for a moment, and he almost stopped the vehicle so he could gather her in his arms again.

"Don't beat yourself up over it," Joshua said instead.

She didn't even look like she was listening to him, though.

"Junior always had a quick answer for everything," she said, staring through the windshield, even though there was nothing out there to be seen. "I knew he loved to flatter and tease. I just never knew he outright lied. I mean, of course I found out when they told me he'd set up the fake wedding thing. But the earrings are almost worse. There was no need to lie to me there. I would have still treasured them if he'd told me they were costume jewelry."

"Junior probably liked giving them to you better if you thought they were worth more, though," Joshua said. "He liked to exaggerate and live the good life."

Just like me, Joshua heard the words in his mind, and the revelation shocked him. He had not tricked anyone into marrying him, but he had certainly used his banter to make women think he was more impressive than he was. He'd hand them a wildflower from the fields and make it seem like an expensive hothouse bloom. Like Junior, he liked to think the other person was happier that way. But it wasn't true. Something humble was not something grand. He was only a step or two behind Junior in sliding the truth to make the moment sound better. Fortunately, God had taken him in hand. *Thank You, Lord, even in my unwillingness, You're dragging me along. Thank You. Don't ever let me mislead anyone.*

Suddenly, being a stodgy bachelor didn't sound so bad. Maybe having the truth in his heart and on his tongue was worth being a dull party guy. At least he wouldn't leave any victims in his wake. It occurred to him suddenly that it would mean others could trust him more. He'd never looked at that side of things before; he'd just always been sure he couldn't trust anyone else.

Joshua drove the pickup out of the medical-center parking lot and onto one of the main roads in Miles City. There was a department store a few blocks from where they were, and the place had a good selection of children's shoes. They could probably even get some jeans and T-shirts for Tommy.

Fifteen minutes later, the three of them were standing in the children's shoe section of a store. Tommy had picked up a pair of sneakers that lit up around the soles when you walked in them. He had pushed the button to see the lights play on the display model.

"The sizes don't go wide enough," a young sales clerk was saying. He'd already measured Tommy's feet.

"How about shoes with bells?" Joshua asked when he saw the longing on Tommy's face as he watched the flashing shoes on the rack.

"I don't think they make anything like that in the size he needs, either," the clerk said. "If they do, I haven't seen them in our stock."

"So, there are just white ones?" Emma asked as she wrinkled her nose in thought. "No blinking stars or anything?"

The clerk shook his head. "We do have some pink ones that have a rim of fur around the opening."

"Pink?" Joshua said and shook his head decisively. "For girls."

Tommy had turned to watch him, and when Joshua looked down, the boy started shaking his head just as emphatically as Joshua had done.

"That's my boy," Joshua said.

"Get for Rosie?" Tommy asked then, his eyes hopeful.

"Rosie can get her own shoes," Joshua said. Maybe Max had been right, and he and Tommy were destined to always watch out for their damsels.

"Rosie princess," Tommy said with a wistful look in his eyes.

"Yes, she is," Joshua agreed. "If you want to get her a present, though, I know she likes chocolate candy bars."

"Me get?" Tommy asked excitedly.

Joshua nodded. "Remind me, and we'll get one at the store, champ."

"Me champ?" Tommy asked, looking up at Joshua.

"You're the best champ," Joshua told him firmly.

"Ah," the sales clerk said, and his face lit up. "We just got in some sneakers that I think you might like. Let me go in the back and see if we have the right size."

Emma started looking at the stickers on the bottom of the shoes when the clerk was gone. "These prices are pretty good. I can pay for them."

"I could put them on my credit card," Joshua said, although he figured that wouldn't satisfy her. He didn't think today was the best time to give her that cigar box, but he'd have to find a good time to do so before she spent her last penny.

The clerk returned carrying a shoebox.

"Let's try these," he said as he turned to Tommy and pulled out a pair of sports sneakers. A blue racing strip went down the side of the shoe, and the word *CHAMP* was printed across the heel.

"Me champ," Tommy said, smiling and nodding as he lifted his foot and slipped it into the shoe that the clerk held ready for him.

"They are a running shoe," the clerk said, "but Tommy moves fast enough for them."

Emma peeked at the bottom of the other shoe and nodded before turning to Joshua. "Shall we take them?"

"What do you think, Tommy?" Joshua asked the boy. "Would you like these shoes?"

Tommy beamed and nodded.

"Good enough for me," Joshua said to Emma.

"How much is the total due?" Emma asked the clerk as she reached down and opened her purse. She pulled out a twenty dollar bill and a five dollar bill.

"We have a discount today," the clerk said. "They're $19.99."

The clerk walked over to a cash register, and Emma followed him. She gave him the twenty-dollar bill, and he gave her a penny back along with a receipt.

Joshua could see the flash of satisfaction on Emma's face when she paid for her brother's shoes.

They started to exit the store when Joshua saw a pile of boys' jeans. He managed to grab two pairs for Tommy without upsetting Emma and, at the register, Joshua added three nearby T-shirts—one red, one yellow, and one dark blue. Emma refused to do any shopping for herself, though, and he knew she was tired so he agreed.

"A stop at the grocery store, and we'll head home," Joshua said as they left the building.

Emma was so tired that she opted to stay in the pickup while Joshua and Tommy went shopping for food. It didn't take them long. Tommy picked out one large chocolate candy bar and ten packages of cookies, some vanilla sandwich ones, some marshmallow-filled ones, and a selection of wafer bars and shortbread.

Joshua got three packages of ready-to-eat barbeque pulled pork and hamburger buns for tonight as well as a half-dozen bags of salad and three frozen pans of meat lasagna for the future. At the last minute, Tommy reminded him about the ice cream and pickles, so he piled that in the cart, as well. That would cover them for supper and dessert. As tired as Emma was, she should be resting with her feet up or taking a nap instead of cooking when they got home.

Joshua hurried the cart and Tommy back to the pickup and then stopped when he glanced inside. Emma was curled up against the passenger side window, and she was sleeping.

"Quiet," Joshua instructed Tommy in a whisper. "Emma's sleeping."

The boy nodded, and Joshua set the groceries in the back of the pickup so he could lift Tommy into the cab from the driver's side. The boy carefully slid across the seat so he would not wake his sister.

"Attaboy," Joshua said softly, and Tommy beamed.

Joshua covered up the groceries with the tarp he kept in the truck bed. It was cold enough outside that even the ice cream would do fine. Then he climbed in and backed up his vehicle as smoothly as he could and turned around so they could head back to the ranch.

"Going home?" Tommy asked quietly.

Joshua nodded.

Tommy looked happy, and Joshua noticed that he felt pretty good, too. They were going home together. If someone didn't know better, they would look like an ordinary family heading to their house. He looked over at Emma again.

"Yes, we are going home," he said softly.

* * *

Emma felt the disruption in her sleep when she heard the word *home*. For a long time that word conjured up the picture of her trailer, but now she saw in her mind the bunkhouse at the Rosen Ranch. She was surprised that it made her feel good to think of her comfortable bed there and the good memories she already had of the place. She supposed she should worry about where home was going to be after she had her baby, but her mind just seemed to drift. Soon the steady purr of the engine lulled her back to sleep.

The next thing she knew, she was waking up and they were back in front of the main house of the ranch. She straightened up and rubbed her eyes. Joshua was looking over at her.

"I thought we'd unload here before going to the bunkhouse," Joshua said. "With everyone sleeping, it seemed the best."

He smiled then, and Emma looked down at Tommy snuggled against her side, curled up as usual. She saw something shiny and leaned over so she could see it better.

"Oh, no," Emma said. "Tommy's almost melted that candy bar. I didn't know he had it in his hands."

Fortunately, there was no smear of chocolate anywhere so the inside hadn't escaped. The heat of his fingers had softened it some, though, and it drooped on the ends. Emma gently slipped the bar away from him. "He should have left it in the back with the other groceries. The temperature is too cold outside to bother it."

Joshua pulled out a large white handkerchief from somewhere and held it out so Emma could lay the candy bar on top of it.

"Tommy wants to be sure no one gives the candy bar to Rosie until he can do the honors," Joshua said with a smile on his face as he tucked the handkerchief around the candy. "He's truly smitten, and every man wants to please his sweetheart."

"He's only seven," Emma protested.

"Prime time for falling in love," Joshua said as he opened his door. "Which you would know if you were a little boy."

"Well, I'm not," Emma said and then gasped.

Joshua had started to step down from the cab, but he returned his leg to the seat and was sitting beside her again. "A pain?"

"No, just the usual kick," Emma said. "I guess the baby wants me to know it's not a boy."

"Or maybe it wants you to know it is a boy," Joshua said, and then he was silent for a bit. "Did the doctor tell you if it was going to be a boy or a girl?"

Rosie shook her head. "She asked if I wanted to know, and I said no." She looked over at Joshua. "I know the sex of my baby wouldn't make a difference in what I would get from Eli's ranch if I had the baby take a DNA test, but I still don't think I'll have that test. I just can't decide."

"No need to decide yet," Joshua said. "The will gives you a little time."

Emma hesitated and then started to talk about it. "I suppose people think I'm strange for not putting my hat in the ring to get some of the Rosen Ranch, but I'm just not sure it's right."

"Eli wanted his grandchildren to have good lives," Joshua said. "Given that, it's as right as it can be."

Emma tried to absorb that. "My stepfather is my

baby's grandfather, too—legally, anyways—and he probably doesn't even want to know if the baby is born. He certainly won't be planning to worry about him or her financially."

"Men can be very different," Joshua said. "Old Eli wasn't a soft man, but he had a side to him. He valued his family, no matter what they did. Junior broke his heart. All he had left were the grandchildren. Eli's bloodline was what mattered at the end of his life."

Emma nodded. "I already put Junior's name on the clinic form as the baby's father. I'm not trying to say Eli isn't grandfather to my baby. I just feel funny taking any money for that."

Suddenly, Emma heard the sound of the front door of the house opening, and a girlish squeal split the air.

"You're home," Rosie screamed in excitement as she stood in the doorway and jumped up and down.

Emma couldn't help but smile as she waited for Joshua to walk around and help her step down from the pickup. She couldn't remember the last time anyone had greeted her so enthusiastically. Rosie clearly wasn't concerned about who belonged on the ranch and who didn't. She applauded everyone.

Emma looked at the house as she started to walk toward it. Someone had scraped the snow out of the flower beds. She guessed someone—Bailey, most likely—was going to prepare the beds for a planting of bulbs that would bloom later in the spring. It was the adults in this house that would know Emma didn't belong.

Families were tended like those bulbs would be. Any seeds that wandered into those flower beds would be plucked out before they could take root. It was only right. But Emma didn't want to be plucked from anywhere. She had her place, and she would go back to it, even if it wasn't nearly as nice as this ranch. She wondered suddenly, though, what her child would think of that when they were grown. Would they feel she had cheated them out of something?

Chapter Eight

After Joshua kicked off his boots on the doormat, he took the melted candy bar into the kitchen without anyone seeing what he held in his handkerchief. In his stocking feet, Tommy followed anxiously behind him.

Joshua looked around to be sure no one was sitting at the kitchen table. Then he waited a second in case someone was standing elsewhere by some cabinet. The clock on the wall ticked loudly. The linoleum on the floor was highly polished. A rack of dishes was drying on the counter by the sink. All was as it should be.

"Be okay?" Tommy asked in a stage whisper. "Me—no want chocolate to—" Tommy made motions with his hands to mimic melting.

"In a few minutes, it should be just fine," Joshua said as he walked over to the refrigerator and opened the freezer compartment. "It's not your fault. I should have realized what was happening."

Tommy looked shocked. "Not you. Me—Tommy did bad."

"We're friends," Joshua said as he laid the handkerchief-wrapped candy bar out flat on top of a package of frozen steaks. "You and me, we help each other out. I don't mind taking the blame. I have big shoulders. You can count on me."

You can trust me, Joshua thought to himself.

Tommy grinned, and his eyes sparkled. "Me Joshua friend. You take blame. Big shoulders. Good. Tommy shoulders small."

"That's right," Joshua said with a chuckle as he patted the boy on his shoulder and got a giggle in return. "Now, let's go get the rest of the groceries and put them away."

Tommy nodded and trailed out of the kitchen behind Joshua.

Joshua walked into the living room with nothing on his mind and felt the change in the air immediately. Something had gone wrong, and he didn't know what it was. The overstuffed chairs were all in the same place, facing the worn couch. The sunlight still streamed in from the large-paned windows on the right. But Emma sat there in one of the chairs with a stricken expression on her face and her dry hands down at her side, tucked close to the arms of the chair. Bailey Rosen was sitting in the chair across from her, the baby held up against her shoulder. She was looking down at the baby and so didn't seem to have noticed Emma's expression. Soft voices came from Rosie's room, likely from the girl and Mrs. Hargrove.

Not knowing what else to do, Joshua walked over to stand beside the chair where Emma was sitting. If there was a major problem, he knew whose corner he would be in.

"Feel another kick?" Joshua asked softly as he pulled a wooden chair close to where Emma sat. He knew the baby's movements would not make her look like this, but he needed to start somewhere. He didn't have time to sit down before she started to talk.

"No, I…" Emma muttered hesitantly and glanced over at Bailey as though she didn't want the other woman to hear what she had to say. "I, uh… I opened the letter about Tommy from my stepfather."

Emma stopped then, and Joshua knew any talking was an effort for her. She just looked up at him, her chestnut curls falling as she tilted her face backward. Her hazel eyes seemed to beg him for something important, and he almost reached down and took her in his arms. He didn't have a chance to move, though, because she pulled a white sheet of paper out of the chair beside her and held it out to him in a trembling hand.

He accepted it and discovered a piece of ruled school paper that might have been torn out of one of Tommy's notebooks. It was written in ink and had a full proper date at the top of the page so it looked legal enough. In rounded cursive writing it said.

I, Harry Smitt, until today raised Tommy Watkins-Smitt, though he was no blood relation to me and not formally adopted, for some four years since I married his mother, Ruth Watkins. She is now dead, and I can no longer care for Tommy so I give him solely into the care of—

"Oh," Joshua saw it, and then he understood.

He sank down to the straight-backed chair and looked over at Emma.

"What am I going to do?" she wailed.

"What's wrong?" Bailey asked as she looked up from her baby at Emma's cry.

Tears streaked down Emma's cheeks. "It's a misunderstanding. Me and my pride. I should have told my stepfather about Junior. It's all my fault."

"Is there anything I can do to help?" Bailey offered, and that only made Emma's tears flow faster.

"It's not your problem," Emma said. "Not by rights. It's just—" She turned to Joshua. "Will you read it aloud?"

Joshua heard footsteps at the door coming into the porch off the kitchen. "Let's wait for Mark. He'll want to hear this, too."

No one said a word until the other man walked into the living room.

"You'll want to sit down for this," Joshua said to his friend. Then Joshua noticed that Tommy had come into the living room, too, so he turned to him. "Why don't you go tell Rosie about your new T-shirts?"

"Okay," Tommy said and walked to the back of the house where Mrs. Hargrove and Rosie were.

Joshua read aloud the first part of the notice, and then he got to the part that was troublesome. "I can no longer care for Tommy so I give him solely into the care of Mr. and Mrs. Junior Rosen."

"He meant me," Emma protested softly. "I didn't want him to know what a fool I'd been so he thought that was me. No one would expect the two of you to do anything."

"Technically, it's only Bailey that could do anything at this point," Joshua noted in the silence that followed. "Of course, I'm not sure how legal the entire note is anyway. But currently she is Mrs. Junior Rosen."

"We need an attorney to help us figure this out," Mark said. "I'm sure there's a solution."

"We did get Emma's stepfather's location—where

he's moving to in Florida," Joshua mentioned. "I'd have to go through my glove compartment, but I wrote it down on the back of a receipt."

"I wondered why you asked him where they were going," Emma said. "How did you know he'd pull something like this?"

"I didn't," Joshua said. He should have suspected something, but truthfully her stepfather hadn't meant to be tricky. He was just being very official. Joshua glanced over and noted that the color in Emma's face was better.

"I'll do anything I can to help," Bailey said as she gave Emma a sympathetic nod. "You told me what your stepfather was up to the other day. No one wants Tommy to go into a home like he was planning."

"I bet Gabe could give us some direction," Mark said. "He keeps reminding us he's a Rosen. Let him use that fancy law degree of his for more than helping landlords evict their tenants."

"He doesn't do evictions anymore," Bailey said and then added, "Probably not enough excitement for him."

Joshua nodded. Regardless of what kind of cases he handled, Gabe Rosen was a good attorney. And he was the only genuine adult Rosen around since he was Eli's nephew and Junior's cousin. He might as well face the problems with them.

"We can ask him to come for supper tonight," Mark said. "That's a good time to talk to him."

"I don't know what we have to eat," Bailey looked doubtful.

Joshua shrugged. "If you're not concerned with being fancy, I bought several big frozen pans of lasagna when we were in Miles City. We can use one of those, and I got lots of bags of salad fixings."

"I can make some garlic bread knots," Emma offered shyly. "They're easy to do, and people love them. That is, if you have dry yeast?"

"I believe we do," Bailey said. "Back in the cupboard behind the oatmeal."

"You make yeast breads?" Mark asked Emma with a hint of wonder in his voice. "The old-fashioned way? We used to sit and talk about homemade bread when I was overseas in the Army."

Emma nodded.

"I love you," Mark said dramatically.

Emma giggled. Bailey frowned.

"Hey," Joshua protested. "You already have a sweetheart."

"Yes, but can she bake bread?" Mark teased as he leaned down to kiss Bailey on the lips.

Joshua thought the kiss went on longer than it needed to since there were other people around. And then he began to wonder if anyone would notice if he kissed Emma right now. He wasn't quite sure why he had such a strong urge to do just that. Maybe because it would make up for the kiss that had happened at Max's store with the bird. Emma was looking at the other couple with a wistful expression that tugged at his heart. Then he realized he felt the same way, wanting something—and then, suddenly the kiss was over, and Joshua had lost the moment. He'd been too slow.

"If Gabe is coming, we better double the bread recipe," Mark said then with a smile still on his face. "I seem to recall he could eat enough for two."

Joshua frowned. "Remember Emma is pregnant. She can't be slaving over a hot stove all day."

"Oh, there's nothing to it," Emma said with a wave of her hands.

"Well, I'll help you, then," Joshua declared stoutly. He hoped she wasn't planning to lift anything. She might not realize that the ranch bought their flour in fifty-pound bags.

"It's settled, then," Bailey said with a decided nod. "We'll ask Gabe for supper. He hasn't seen the baby yet, and he'll want to do that, too."

Rosie came rushing out of the back bedroom with Tommy trailing behind her.

"Tommy has a present for me," she exclaimed in high excitement. "He told me. It's wrapped and everything!"

Joshua watched Tommy's face glow until it was bright pink. The boy hurried over to Joshua's chair and stood beside him as though he didn't know what to do next.

"Me need your shoulders," Tommy whispered next to Joshua's ears. "I said *wrapping*." Tommy made a flying-away motion with his hands. "Why?"

"It's not your fault and, remember, my shoulders are big." Joshua wasn't sure if Tommy meant his tongue got away with him, but Joshua knew how that could happen. He looked over at Emma who was watching the two of them.

"You have any pens?" he asked.

Emma opened her purse and found a couple that she passed to him.

Joshua nodded his thanks and took Tommy by the hand into the kitchen. Once there, he sat Tommy at the round table and went to the freezer to retrieve the square white handkerchief that was wrapped around the candy bar.

"Draw a picture on this," Joshua said as he spread the handkerchief out on the table and set down the two pens. "A blue and a red. It's a challenge, but you're the champ, and you can do it."

Tommy took the pens, a determined look on his face, and a charming stick-figure picture began to emerge of Rosie talking to the bird in the cage. Then Tommy added a whole series of kisses in red ink floating up from the bird to the top of the handkerchief. It was whimsical and obviously heartfelt.

Tommy finished, and Joshua checked the clock behind the refrigerator. "Five minutes. That's great timing." He retrieved the candy bar and slapped Tommy on the back. "Let's get this present wrapped and presented to the lady."

"Rosie lady?" Tommy asked.

Joshua chuckled. "I guess so."

Joshua had to help Tommy knot the handkerchief around the candy bar so the kisses and Rosie and the bird were all visible. Then the boy carefully and proudly carried his gift back into the living room.

Rosie's squeal did the present justice. Like a perfect lady, she was delighted and insisted she would have to take the handkerchief over to the bunkhouse after supper so that Cupid could see his picture. "And I love chocolate!"

Tommy beamed.

Joshua had to admit to a teary eye himself, just watching the boy.

"Maybe you should bring the bird over here so I can

meet him," Bailey said to her daughter. "Ask the nice man who owns him if he can do that."

Rosie gasped. "No one *owns* Cupid. You can't own a friend."

"His caretaker, then," Bailey adjusted her request.

Rosie nodded. "We shouldn't let Cupid see the baby, though. Cupid shoots arrows at people."

"Oh," Bailey said as she looked up at Mark with worry in her eyes. "Someone is shooting arrows?"

"Rosie knows about the other Cupid," Mark said diplomatically. "The bird Cupid can't shoot anyone." Mark squatted down so he was nose-to-nose with Rosie. "Think about it. How could that bird shoot an arrow?"

Rosie frowned and then smiled. "He can't. He doesn't have any arms."

"That's right," Mark said as he stood up.

"Maybe he shoots the arrows with his feet, though," Rosie protested after a few seconds. "He has awful big toes."

Mark just looked at his new daughter and smiled. "You'd make a good general in the Army. Never underestimate the enemy."

Rosie nodded emphatically. "I won't."

"But I don't think he can shoot arrows with his toes, either," Mark assured her.

"Okay," Rosie said.

Joshua could feel Tommy as the boy stood beside him still vibrating with excitement. Tommy listened to Rosie unfurl her dramas like they were absolutely true and brilliant. Joshua supposed young love was always like that.

Joshua reached over now and put his hand on Emma's arm as she sat in the chair. She wasn't likely to spin fanciful tales like Rosie did, but she did take the weight of the world on her back and stubbornly refused help to lift it.

"What do I need to have this afternoon to help you make bread?" he asked Emma in a low murmur as he watched Tommy and Rosie go into the back of the house. Bailey followed them.

"You're really going to help?" she asked.

He nodded.

"Let him." Bailey turned around in the hall and instructed Emma.

"Okay," Emma said to Joshua with a grin. "Bring an apron. And leave your cowboy hat behind."

"She's letting you off easy," Mark said as he stood and followed Bailey down the hall.

"Yes, she is." Joshua nodded. He would have done a lot more for Emma if she'd only known it. Of course, he had no way to get an apron. There were none in the bunkhouse. But they did have a few large square cotton dish towels that he could tie around his waist. That would have to do.

It was only one o'clock in the afternoon, but Joshua figured their trip to Miles City had made them all weary.

"It might do you good to have a nap," Joshua said.

"Can't," Emma said with a yawn. "Tommy."

"I can see to Tommy," Joshua said. "He can come check the cows with me if he doesn't want a nap of his own."

"Really?" Emma asked as she fought back another yawn.

"Tommy's my buddy," Joshua said as he walked over to get Emma's coat. "I don't mind having him around."

"Then, I will take a nap," Emma said as she started to get up from the chair. By then Joshua was there, and he helped her into her coat.

"Wake me up by two," she said as she started to walk toward the door.

"Will do," Joshua assured her, and he held her arm as they exited the house and strolled over to the bunkhouse.

She fussed about him helping her up the steps and into the bunkhouse, but he didn't pay any mind to it. He was only willing to let her go when they stood before the door to her private room.

"Two o'clock," Emma reminded him.

"You can count on me," Joshua assured her.

Then she walked through the door, and Joshua felt his chest expand. He felt good when he could take care of Emma, and he didn't want it to be limited to helping her with baking. He wanted her to trust him with all of her problems. That realization spun him around. What was he thinking? This was usually the time in his dating relationships when he'd look for an exit. He never wanted anyone to depend on him because, sooner or later, they would want him to trust them the same way. And that could never happen. But this was Emma, something inside him protested. He didn't want to say goodbye to Emma.

Emma was glad she had Joshua's help with the garlic knots. He was the one who found the yeast behind a box of cereal in the top cabinet over the stove. And he brought down the big canister of flour. Maybe it was because he was so busy that he was mostly quiet. It was no matter. She was at peace. She'd walked back over to the main house before Joshua and Tommy were back from checking on the cows and she had stopped several times to appreciate where she was. The ground was still frozen, but there was very little snow scattered around. The temperature was a little warmer than it had been, too. The views were not nearly as majestic as those at her mountain home, she decided, but the ranch looked prosperous and well cared for.

"You just keep sitting at the table," Joshua said after he got the flour from some place in the bottom cupboards. "I'll be the gofer guy."

"This kitchen isn't set up for baking, is it?" Emma said with a frown. The rest of the ranch seemed so functional; she would expect that here, too. But nothing was easy to get to. The room itself was fine with clear light, lots of cupboards and counters. It was the organization that was lacking.

"It was set up to suit Eli," Joshua said, and then he thought a minute. "Maybe even set up to please his wife, and she's been gone for decades. It's been a long time since anyone cared where anything was in here."

"Bailey doesn't cook?" Emma asked.

"I don't think she felt it was her right to change things," Joshua said thoughtfully. "At least not while Eli was still alive."

Emma wondered what it was like to have that strong of a sense of family so that the older generation still had a say in one's decisions.

"What's next?" Joshua asked.

Emma noticed that he had taken his hat off after coming in through the porch, and he'd tied an old dish towel around his waist so he sort of looked like a chef.

"Do you have the recipe?" Joshua looked around, a little nervously, she thought.

"It's up here," Emma said with a tap to her head. "I learned how to make the knots from my mother."

"Really, like a family recipe?" Joshua sounded impressed.

"I guess you could call it that," Emma said. "My mother learned to make them from her mother. And someday I'll teach—" She broke off. She didn't want to sound like one of those pregnant women who go on and on about what they were going to do with their genius babies once they were out of the womb.

"You'll teach little 'night, night'," Joshua finished for her, looking so eager that he almost sounded like one of those women.

Emma swallowed and turned her attention back to the task at hand. "I'll have to stand by the stove while I get the yeast mixture ready, but I'm happy to sit when I can."

She was grateful for the change of conversation. The kitchen had gotten warm for a bit there, and she wasn't sure why.

"You didn't already turn on the stove, did you?" she asked.

Joshua shook his head. "Don't even know what temperature you need."

"Okay, then. That's good," Emma said as she moved the empty pan in front of her to precisely the right spot.

"How's that ankle doing?" Joshua asked as he brought a bag of sugar to the table.

"Practically as good as new," she said and picked up a measuring cup and set to work.

Emma felt more comfortable as she worked on the

bread. After she set the bread to rise the first time, Joshua told her stories from his childhood. He'd already told her about being taken from his parents by Child Protective Services when he was young, but she was amazed at the number of homes he'd been in for a few months here and a year there. He made light of the chaos—once losing every pair of shoes he owned—but she wondered all the same. When the bread was ready to work, he teased a few laughs out of her as he helped her with the rolling pin. Together they made the thick strands to loop into knots. He even melted the butter and helped brush the knots before they were put into the oven.

By the time the garlic knots were browned and ready to come out of the oven, the lasagna had also cooked. In the last minutes of the preparation, Emma had convinced Joshua she was able to stand at the stove long enough to make a large saucepan of chocolate pudding for Rosie.

"You're going to get kissed awake tomorrow morning, too, if you're not careful," Joshua teased her. "Rosie has wanted some good chocolate pudding for weeks now."

"Good pudding isn't too much to ask of life," Emma said as Rosie burst through the kitchen door with Tommy in her wake.

"You made it," Rosie exclaimed as she put her hand to her heart. "My chocolate pudding. You're the best princess ever."

Then Rosie ran over to Emma and wrapped her arms around her as much as she could given the size of Emma's middle.

"I'm happy to do it." Emma blinked back a tear as

she patted the girl's head. Emma decided it was true that a woman's emotions went all over the place when she was pregnant. She'd never been a watering pot, not in all of her life until now. She'd almost cried when Joshua talked about being shuffled all over the place as he grew up, and now another tear showed up when Rosie was so happy.

"Well, we better get the table set," Emma said finally, and Rosie and Tommy went over to the stack of plates and silverware that Joshua had laid out. Mark came in to add a leaf to the kitchen table. A soft knock at the front door revealed Max was there with his bird in the covered cage. He set the bird on a small table by the far window and stood in the doorway to the kitchen, watching the action.

By the time the table was set, Gabe was there, too, and everyone else was getting ready to sit down. Gabe, still in a suit and tie from work, was given the chair at the head of the table. Mrs. Hargrove, Max, Rosie and Tommy filed in on the right side of the table; Mark, Bailey, Joshua and Emma sat on the other.

Joshua and Mark put the food on the table, except for the bowl of chocolate pudding that needed to cool some.

"Will you pray for us, Gabe?" Bailey asked the man respectfully.

Emma decided that was a regular request as he didn't look the least surprised.

"Lord, we thank You for Your bounty and for the friends and family with whom we share it," Gabe said. "Amen."

There was a moment of silence after the prayer, and then Joshua picked up the platter of garlic knots and held it while he circled it around the table so the others could smell the scents without being close enough to take one.

"Hey," Mark protested.

"I will politely pass the knots to everyone," Joshua said. "But first we need to thank the woman who baked them—Emma Smitt!"

Emma knew she'd turned pink. "Others helped."

"Just me," Joshua said as he passed the platter.

Mark took two knots for his plate before relinquishing the platter to Bailey. Then he took one bite, and a look of bliss came over his face. "I have to—"

"You can't propose again," Joshua interrupted with emphasis.

A slow grin spread over Mark's face. "Maybe not, but I can sure give advice to any slow starters."

"Who slow?" Tommy asked from across the table with a worried frown on his forehead.

"No one is," Emma said firmly. The people here probably didn't know that *slow* was one of the trigger words for children with Down syndrome. They weren't slow. Tommy certainly wasn't. They were just unique.

Tommy still looked uncertain until Joshua leaned over toward him.

"Not you, champ," Joshua whispered. "He meant me."

"You slow?" Tommy asked in surprise.

"He thinks I am about some things," Joshua admitted.

By that time, all of the dishes were being passed around, and Emma had a few minutes of calm. She had just realized that Tommy got more assurance from Joshua than he did from her. She supposed a boy needed a man to tell him all was right with the world, but Emma was all Tommy had for now. The two of them had slipped into this situation at the ranch so easily, but the truth was they weren't staying. Once the baby came, she would need to move back to the trailer. Of course, there were no jobs there so she'd need to rent an apartment elsewhere.

It was hard to be serious tonight, though, not while everyone was smacking their lips over the garlic knots, and Tommy and Rosie were giggling as they tried to walk the knots across their plates like they were soldiers.

"My mother used to call them garlic *hugs* rather than *knots*," Emma said to the children. "They're a bread of peace, not war."

"I'll second that," Joshua said with a sigh of contentment. "Who could think of going to battle when they had a few of those garlic hugs to feast on?"

"And there's pudding," Rosie added with a glance at her mother. "If I'm a good girl and eat all my supper."

"Did you hide anything in your napkin?" Bailey asked as she looked at her daughter.

Rosie reluctantly opened her napkin. "Just that tiny bit of lettuce that is too hard to eat. I think it is spinach."

"There's no spinach in the salad tonight," Joshua said. Everyone knew what Rosie thought of spinach.

"Would you like it, then?" Rosie asked hopefully as she held out the offensive piece of lettuce.

"I think that's red cabbage," Joshua said as he put the morsel beside his plate.

"See," Rosie said and turned to her mother, lifting her plate in triumph. "All gone."

"I don't think that's quite fair," Bailey said. "But since Emma made the pudding with you in mind, you can have some for dessert."

Rosie smiled and looked cherubic.

Tommy looked pleased, too, as he looked over at Joshua. "You shoulders for Rosie, too?"

Joshua chuckled softly. "I guess so."

"Good," Tommy said.

Emma wasn't quite sure what Tommy had asked, but she realized it had something to do with Joshua always coming to the rescue for people. He did it in big things and small things. She'd thought it was just her situation that had bothered him enough to try and rescue her, but it happened in other ways for other people all the time.

Everyone had two bowls of warm chocolate pudding, even Rosie who also requested and was granted the honor of scraping every lick of pudding from the pan in which it had been cooked.

Rosie had chocolate pudding on her chin. Tommy had managed to smear some on his eyebrow. Mrs. Hargrove announced that both of them needed to come with her and clean their faces. Max decided to retire to the living room to visit with Cupid for a few minutes. Bailey and Mark stood up to put the dishes in the sink.

"We'll wash them later," Mark said as the two of them quickly moved the dishes and sat back down at the table. "After we talk about the letter."

The five adults were all silent for a moment after they were all seated, and Gabe began.

"Mark explained the situation," Gabe said with a glance to Emma. "We all understand how the mistake was made. I have a few questions before I can advise on how we should proceed."

Emma noticed he said *we* and she felt wrapped in support.

"First, Emma," Gabe began, "do you have any document that shows you are Tommy's sister?"

"I'm not sure I am his sister, legally," she admitted. "Our mothers both married the same man. My mother first and then Tommy's. Both of our mothers died. Tommy and I have always considered ourselves brother and sister, but we have no blood tie."

"I see," Gabe said and frowned.

Joshua moved his chair closer to her, and Emma saw him reach out a hand to her. She took it gratefully. "Is that a problem—us not having a blood tie?"

"Probably what it means is that we have to go through CPS—Child Protective Services," Gabe said thoughtfully. "I've had cases with them, and they're not unreasonable."

"Can we just explain about the confusion on my name?" Emma asked.

"I don't think what your stepfather wrote would be legal, anyway," Gabe said. "It wasn't notarized, and we may not be able to find him to verify it."

"I'll go to Florida personally," Joshua offered.

"We may still need to go through CPS," Gabe said. "So that's how we should prepare."

"How's that?" Emma asked, taking a firmer grip on Joshua's hand. "I love Tommy. I'm willing to take care of him. He wants to be with me."

"But can you take care of him?" Gabe asked gently. "That's what CPS will want to know. He has a special...situation, I guess we'll call it. Can you see to what he needs?"

"I'll do whatever I have to do," Emma promised.

"But, as I understand it, you don't have a job," Gabe continued. "I heard Eli's will and your refusal to have the DNA test he required to get some of his ranch." Gabe held up a hand. "That's your right. I'm not questioning that. I'm just saying that the CPS folks will want to know how you're going to provide for Tommy. Do you have any other income?"

Emma closed her eyes. "I have a small monthly check of three hundred and fifty dollars that comes."

Emma hated to mention that money from Junior.

"That will help," Gabe said thoughtfully. "And you can probably qualify for some welfare with Tommy and the baby. You'd likely get health insurance, too. Can you verify those checks? Where do they come from?"

Emma felt her mind scramble for the answer. "Do you need to know that?"

"If we want them to count," Gabe said. "And they might make a difference with CPS—with those checks and the fact that you already own your trailer—you do own your trailer?"

"I do," Emma answered and then stopped in defeat. She figured those checks were a mistake in some accounting system. No one would be sending them now that Junior was gone.

"I send the checks," Bailey said quietly from her corner of the table. "I mean, they come from the ranch expenses. They were set up automatically by Junior, and I haven't stopped them." Bailey cleared her throat. "And I won't stop them. If anything, we can talk about making them bigger."

"Oh," Emma stared at Bailey who was looking down at the table as though she didn't want to meet Emma's gaze, either. "I...well, thank you."

Bailey still didn't raise her eyes. "It's the least I can do." Bailey paused, and it was so quiet they could have heard a pin drop. It was like everyone knew more was coming. "It was my fault Junior was out tomcatting around the countryside."

Mark moved his chair closer to Bailey and put his arm around her.

"No, I'm the one to blame," Emma protested.

Out of the corner of her eye, it looked like Joshua moved his chair closer, but maybe he just wanted to reach something.

"Junior loved you," Bailey whispered, her voice tight. Her eyes rose up to meet Emma's and wouldn't let go. "I know he cared for you. I was never the wife he wanted. That's why he turned to someone else."

Emma gasped. Bailey had it all wrong, and the other woman was starting to cry.

Mark was moving closer still to Bailey. Emma knew she needed to speak the truth before Bailey couldn't hear it for the comfort of his hug, but Emma's throat was dry.

"Those earrings," she finally managed to say. "They're not diamonds at all. The clerk in the jewelry store this morning said they were cubic zirconia."

"Really?" Bailey's tears stopped. She stared at Emma in surprise. Mark stopped with his hug to turn to her, as well.

Emma nodded. "They were as fake as our wedding ceremony. Junior didn't love me. He must have just liked playing the role of a groom."

"I doubt he loved anyone," Joshua said.

"I'm sure he—" Gabe started to protest and then

gave up. "Junior never was too concerned with anyone but himself—that I can accept."

Bailey dried her eyes and looked directly at Emma. "Don't worry about the money. We'll make those checks for whatever amount we need to so that CPS will know you can take care of Tommy."

"That's too much," Emma protested. "I plan to get a job after the baby comes. We'll be fine."

"So do you want me to go ahead and look for your stepfather?" Gabe asked Emma.

"Yes, please," she said. She realized she needed to know how to reach him if she was going to handle Tommy's future.

"Good," Gabe said as he started to get up from the table. "That about finishes the business, then. I'll make a contact with CPS and put out some feelers about our next steps."

"Thank you," Emma said as Joshua stepped over to help her rise.

Joshua held out his arm to Emma and escorted her into the living room, even though now that her ankle was healed she didn't really need any assistance. Still, she thought as she moved a little closer to him, it was nice.

Emma had to convince Joshua that she would prefer to sit in the straight-backed chair rather than the soft living-room chair, but finally everyone was seated, and it was apparent Max had been waiting for the moment to unveil Cupid.

The bird did not disappoint, squawking loudly when the cover was removed and fluffing its feathers like it was getting ready to perform.

"It can't fly," Rosie whispered to her mother as she

scooted closer to Bailey and Mark. "It doesn't have arms."

"A bird only needs wings to fly," Mark instructed her, and Rosie scowled as she studied Cupid more closely.

"It does have wings," Rosie announced and looked to her soon-to-be daddy for approval.

Mark nodded. "Good job."

Cupid had been listening apparently, because he lifted his head and screeched, "Kiss the bird. Kiss the bird."

"Now, Cupid," Max said clearly. "That's not polite. Not everyone wants to kiss a bird."

Cupid cocked his head to the side and looked out at the people.

"Cupid listens," Tommy said in awe as he pointed.

Cupid made a very birdlike snort and then started again, his beady eyes on Tommy. "Kiss the boy. Kiss the boy."

"Kiss me?" Tommy asked as his face lit up with delight.

"You got it, champ," Joshua said as he dived into the space between them to give Tommy a resounding smack on his forehead. "Kiss for you."

Emma watched. Joshua had started everyone. It was a rainfall of kisses. First Mark went over and kissed Tommy on the cheek. Mrs. Hargrove stood up next and kissed the top of Tommy's head. Bailey followed. Even Gabe gave the boy a kiss on his head. Emma stood up and gave her brother both a hug and a kiss. By then Tommy was glowing.

Finally, Rosie was the only one left, and Emma suspected the girl had planned it that way. She walked over to Tommy and kissed him emphatically on his chin, which was as high as she could reach.

Emma worried Tommy might stop breathing he was so beside himself. Then he walked over to where she was sitting and leaned in to whisper to her, "Like Tommy. All like Tommy."

Emma nodded as she held back the tears. She was the only one in the room who knew what this moment meant to her brother. Usually, people were polite and tolerated him. He was the last one to be picked at any kind of a game. He never had other kids come and ask if he could play with them. He had always been on the outside looking in as the other children played.

Now, everyone had celebrated him. They liked him. All Emma could do was hug him and hug him again. She and Tommy sat there as long as they could enjoying the companionship of everyone. But the night finally grew later until Bailey started to yawn. Even Rosie drooped.

"Time to go home," Emma whispered to Joshua, and he nodded.

The stars were out that night, and Tommy wanted to stop and look at them since he had his glasses now and could see the distant orbs. Emma realized that the stars were another discovery for her brother. And she wouldn't have even known he needed glasses if Joshua hadn't figured it out. How many more things would her brother need that she wouldn't realize? For the first time, she understood what she was taking on with Tommy. But there was no choice. He belonged with her. She'd find a way to give him what he needed. She looked over at Joshua as the man was pointing out the constellations to Tommy. She'd just be grateful for what she and her brother had today.

She put her hand on her stomach again. She, Tommy and the baby would be fine. They had friends who liked them, she thought with a smile. She stood like that for a moment until she realized that it wasn't enough. She wanted so much more than that. She wanted to be loved and not by a man like Junior again. She wanted to be loved by a man she respected, a man she could trust. Someone like—she shook her head. No, she could not name him even in her mind.

Chapter Nine

Joshua followed Mark to the empty Durham house early the next morning. The key turned hard in Mark's hand as he opened the place, which Joshua figured was a sure sign of swelling in the wood. As he had suspected, a slight musty smell welled up inside the building when he stepped past the doorway.

"The location's good," Mark said as they both stood there.

The Durham ranch shared a fence with the Rosen back corral, and the accompanying house was within easy walking distance of Bailey's place if a person didn't mind getting their clothes snagged while going through the barbwire fence that stood between the two places. And, if they weren't afraid of the cows in the corral that interrupted the most direct route.

Mark reached over and flipped a light switch in the old-style living room. By then he had stepped onto a small bristle mat by the door and scraped his boots to clear any mud. There was a row of hooks on the wall next to him, and he hung his hat. "I wasn't sure the electricity would still be on. Old man Durham had the place wrapped up and ready to sell a few days after I made my offer."

Joshua noticed the light was weak as it filtered down from the bulbs in the ceiling. They could probably be changed out cheaply enough though even if a man needed to replace the fixtures.

Mark stepped off the mat, and Joshua took his turn at brushing his boots across the gritty bristles to free them of any debris.

"I need to do some work on the doorways," Mark admitted as he glanced around. "The damp from being empty this past winter has started to warp some of the wood. We had a wet winter."

"That's why Mr. Durham went south to Arizona?" Joshua asked, even though he knew the answer. He took the time to walk over to the room's big-paned windows that looked toward the Rosen Ranch. The view wasn't much with the stubble of dead grass showing through what little snow was left.

Mark nodded. "Not sure he will do that again. He said he wasn't much on the desert. Too many lizards and bugs for him. And those wild hogs, he said, were worse than any animal on his place."

Joshua nodded absentmindedly.

"There might be a leak in the roof someplace," he said, looking at the ceiling more critically. It appeared fine, but he wasn't sure. "That damp has to come from someplace."

"Probably comes from the chimney," Mark said. "I noticed earlier the old man didn't have that shut off properly when he left. And then a couple of the windows aren't sealed well enough."

"Could be all of that," Joshua agreed. "The main

selling point for the house is that it is close enough to the Rosen place that, if we put a gate in that fence this side of the barn, a body could walk to Bailey's house from here in ten minutes—maybe less."

Mark grinned. "Worried you'll miss breakfast if you rent the place?"

"Who says I'm renting the place?" Joshua asked.

"Why else would you be worried about the damp?" Mark shot back.

"I haven't decided what I'm doing yet," Joshua admitted as he studied the room he was in. There were some nice walnut bookshelves that showcased the working fireplace that Mark had mentioned. A faded rose couch stood in front of the fireplace with a mahogany coffee table that bore stains from hundreds of hot cups of coffee.

"It's got some dust," Joshua said as his eyes continued their way across the room, noting a few more shelves and a grandfather clock.

"Well, you can't worry about something like that," Mark said with a grimace. "The old man wasn't likely to be much at cleaning house. Not with him still putting in full days with a wheat crop and running cattle like he was."

"Still, neglect is hard on the wood," Joshua said. "So did he move his things to the smaller house you mentioned?"

"He sure did," Mark said as he waved in the direction opposite of the Rosen Ranch. "It was the old foreman's house and nice enough. The furniture that's left here he can't use so it would go with the place…" he paused and gave Joshua a cautious look "…if someone was inclined to rent it."

"The furniture is a bit old," Joshua said.

"It's built to last," Mark responded. "And you can't look a gift horse in the mouth. You might take a bed or two from the bunkhouse, but that's about it. We don't have a spare couch or kitchen table."

Joshua grunted. Then he walked down a short hall and saw four bedrooms. All but one of them had a bed, but none of the mattresses were in good shape. The main bedroom had large windows, though, and if he remembered correctly, Mrs. Durham had planted a dozen lilac bushes on that side of the house decades ago.

"Those bushes still giving off their smell?" Joshua asked.

"Mr. Durham said they've gotten sweeter every year," Mark answered. "If you leave those windows open on a summer night, you sleep like a baby. At least, that's what he told me."

Joshua continued on, looking into the bathroom that was right off the main bedroom. It was clean and in good repair, but that was all that could be said for it. "I don't know about that pink sink and toilet. And a butterfly night-light?"

"Those come from the days of Mrs. Durham," Mark said. "Lots of years ago. There's no need to replace anything, though. It all works. Close your eyes if you can't stand the pink."

Joshua went back into the bedroom and leaned closer to inspect the walls. "Needs a paint job in here, too."

"The whole place could use a paint job," Mark said. "It'll make a good project for us next winter."

"That might not be soon enough." Joshua walked out of the bedroom, down the hall and into the kitchen.

"What's your hurry?" Mark asked as he followed Joshua. "The walls in the bunkhouse need painting, too, and you haven't mentioned them. In fact, they're probably worse."

Joshua decided he liked the kitchen. "Lots of cabinets and cupboards. Do those big cast iron skillets go with it? They'd do for baking pans almost. Corn bread, for sure."

"You aren't planning to cook here, are you?" Mark asked. "I always figured the ranch hand wages came with meals and a bed. No sense in doing your own cooking."

"I might want to have company," Joshua said as he walked over and opened the refrigerator. "This is fairly new. And it has a good freezer to it."

Mark stood there a moment and studied Joshua.

"Any company you have is welcome to join all of us in the main house, you know that," Mark said, a frown on his face. "I wouldn't want you to feel that, if you rent this house, it means you don't have a home with Bailey and me."

Joshua gave Mark a warm smile. "I appreciate that."

Mark kept standing there looking at Joshua until finally he exclaimed, "Why, you old dog—you're thinking of getting married!"

Joshua looked over at the other man in alarm. "Don't say anything to anyone. I want to ask, but I don't know if I can pull it off."

"With the proposal? With that smooth tongue of yours, you won't have any trouble convincing anyone to marry you," Mark said, his eyes sparkling with glee.

"I wouldn't make any assumptions," Joshua said slowly. He hadn't wanted anyone to know, but he supposed everyone would know eventually. "I can't talk like I used to."

"What do you mean?" Mark turned his head and asked. "You're talking now."

"I mean the fancy talking," Joshua explained. "I can't seem to think of the words to shape a compliment even though my heart is appreciating..." he hesitated and then decided that, too, wouldn't be a secret for long "… Emma—I can't sweet-talk Emma."

Mark looked at him dubiously. "Maybe you could get her a bouquet of flowers. The box of Valentine candy I got for Bailey sure helped when I asked the big question."

"She would have said yes if you'd given her a box of river rocks," Joshua mumbled.

"Maybe, but a present can sort of break the ice," Mark said.

"I do have a big box of money that I've been trying to give to Emma, but the time is never right," Joshua confessed.

"Your poker money?" Mark asked. When Joshua nodded, Mark continued. "Well, there you go. That's better than a box of rocks. I've always wondered how much you have in that box."

"Three thousand or so," Joshua said.

"Dollars?" Mark asked in astonishment. "And you kept it in your sock drawer?"

"I didn't want to keep it in the bank," Joshua said. "That's where I kept my regular money. That which I'd earned."

"Well, I can't see any woman turning down that kind of money," Mark said.

Joshua shook his head. "You don't know Emma. She

might not take any of it. She hates what she calls charity—claimed it scarred her as a child, having to accept handouts from people who pitied her. I don't pity her at all. I…uh…admire her."

Mark whistled. "Well, of course you do. That's some woman who would turn down that kind of money."

"Well, her refusing the money is to be expected. She won't take part of the Rosen Ranch, either," Joshua said. "So she doesn't do like most people would when it comes to free money. She'd rather earn her way."

"I kind of get it," Mark said as he looked thoughtful. "That's why I bought this place. I didn't want to live off of Bailey's money, either. We all have our pride."

Joshua nodded and was silent for a bit.

"So, when's the big moment?" Mark finally asked.

Joshua looked up at him. "What moment?"

"When you pop the question," Mark replied. "If I know you, you have a plan. You always have a plan for what's happening. When we do the branding, you have it all worked out. If we're thinking of buying a new piece of equipment, you have it planned as to when it will be paid off. You even plan our wheat fields. You're the planning-est guy I know, and I was in the military where there's a plan for brushing your teeth. So when is it?"

Joshua felt his shoulders shift. "I don't have a plan for this. I know it's not like me, but I haven't even thought about a plan." He looked over at Mark. "That's not good, is it?"

"No, no," Mark said hastily, although he did look worried. "Don't listen to me. No one needs a plan to propose. In fact, it's probably better if it's spontaneous and from the heart."

"I can't find the words," Joshua said glumly.

"You have to go in it with confidence—plan or no plan," Mark said as he stepped over and slapped Joshua on the back. "You'll be fine."

"Yeah, sure," Joshua said. He was lying, but he figured Mark wouldn't call him on it.

"So we're good here?" Mark asked. "You can rent the place tomorrow if you want. I'll give you a cheap price you can afford even on your salary." He laughed at that.

"I'll want it ready for the baby," Joshua said with more assurance. This much he knew. "I can start cleaning it tonight after work."

"We'll spend the afternoon on it," Mark agreed. "Bailey has that Bible-study group meeting at the house then, anyway. We should be able to scrub the place down by the time that's over."

Joshua felt the grin growing on his face. "I'll be glad Emma has a place to bring her baby."

Joshua looked up and saw Mark looking at him curiously again.

"You're going to let her live in the house whether or not she agrees to marry you, aren't you?" Mark asked.

Joshua shrugged. "I don't want to force her into marrying me."

"Don't give up before you even propose," Mark said. "You'd make her a good husband."

Joshua wished he had as much confidence in that statement as Mark did. But he didn't say anything as they started walking back the way they had come. They had to climb over a fence post before they got to the Rosen barn.

"We'll put in a gate right there," Mark said as they

both turned back to look. "Or maybe we should go to the side of the field over there so no one has to walk through the corral."

"I don't think we want Rosie coming up against any angry cows," Joshua agreed with a grin.

"Yeah," Mark said. "We have to protect our animals. She might frighten them to death with imaginary arrows or some kind of a princess wand."

Joshua chuckled. "And Tommy would be right behind her."

"Kids." Mark stood there with him for a minute. "Whoever thought we'd ever be worrying about our kids."

"I know," Joshua said. "And then there are the babies, too."

Joshua felt a well of contentment rise up in him, even though he knew he had no legal right to feel like those children were his.

"We are blessed men," Mark said, and they continued walking across the grounds of the corral. The few head of cattle they saw were busy eating hay and didn't even look up as they went by.

"We might as well go about our business until we've eaten," Mark said. "Then we can start cleaning. If I know Bailey, she'll already be fussing about having everything ready for her Bible-study group. It's important to her."

"Emma and Tommy are still sleeping in," Joshua said. "They were tired out from yesterday and will want to be awake for the Bible study this afternoon."

"Sounds good," Mark said.

Joshua nodded. Having shared his dream with Mark made him feel that the future he was hoping for might actually come true. Emma was the woman for him; he needed to relax and just propose. But he didn't want to rush her. He knew God needed some time to work with Emma so she could see His love. Joshua didn't want to interfere with that. No, the time to propose was not now. Maybe when the baby was here.

For now, it was time to scrub walls and maybe more.

"You know, some of those walls are so faded and dingy that it might be best to just paint them once we've gotten the grime off," Joshua said.

"I'm game for that. We can run into Dry Creek to the hardware store and pick up what paint we need for a few rooms," Mark agreed. "You got any colors in mind?"

Joshua wondered what color Emma would want in her bedroom. Maybe lilac, he thought. He remembered that from the handkerchief that had belonged to her mother. It must have been embroidered lilacs on the corner. The color would look nice with white curtains and it would go with the bushes outside. Maybe she'd like a pale yellow in the kitchen. Joshua felt he should know such things if he was going to ask her to marry him. Then he remembered he didn't know her middle name, either.

Joshua decided he had work to do.

Several hours later, Emma and Tommy stood on the porch in front of Bailey's house. Emma bent down and smoothed her brother's hair down as she gave him a thorough looking over.

"You're handsome today," she told him as she squeezed him in a brief hug.

Tommy shook his head and plucked at the fabric

of the coat their stepfather had given him when they left Missoula.

"Stinks," he complained as he scrunched up his noise.

Emma knew the coat, really more of a jacket, smelled strongly of the cologne their stepfather used. It seemed to get worse at the ranch. She didn't like the scent any more than Tommy did; it held bad memories for them both. Their stepfather got mean when he went places where he used more cologne than he should.

"We need to keep you warm," Emma said as she straightened up. She needed to be practical. "The coat does that."

Tommy nodded with no enthusiasm. "Tommy warm."

Emma took a deep breath. Neither one of them really wanted to be here. Tommy's discomfort was simple, though. Hers was that a Bible study meant interacting with church women and, except for Bailey, the religious women she had encountered since she was old enough to know what charity was were well-dressed and distant as they gave handouts to her and her family, be it food or used clothes or, in rare cases, money for rent. She hated that her family had needed help. Somehow the neediness made her feel less of a person. She didn't want to feel like that again.

Emma lifted her hand up to knock on the door, but Bailey opened it before there was any need to do so. She had a wide grin on her face and baby Lilly in her arms. "Come in. I'm glad you're both here."

"We walked," Tommy said proudly.

"Good for you," Bailey said as she patted him on

the shoulder. "Rosie has some books set up in the back for the two of you."

Tommy walked right in, and Emma slid in behind him. Then she remained standing near the closed door while Tommy, still in his coat, quickly went to find Rosie.

A quick glance around the room showed Emma that, in her blue top with its sparkles and her jeans, she was dressed as well as the other women. No one was scowling at her or looking haughty. Mrs. Hargrove was in one of her gingham housedresses with pockets and a zippered front, which Emma had noticed in the days she'd been here was what the woman normally wore. Her white hair was pulled back into a tidy bun. The older woman looked comfortable but not fashionable. Emma doubted she had a mean bone in her body, and it didn't appear she had any airs to her, either.

Bailey stepped closer to Emma. "Let me take your coat."

"Thank you." Emma pulled the garment off.

Bailey then guided her a little farther into the room so that she faced the other women.

"Let me introduce you," Bailey said and started around. Emma tried to remember the names.

There was Doris June, who was Mrs. Hargrove's daughter, a middle-aged woman who looked happy and was dressed in a polyester pantsuit. She stood up to shake Emma's hand. "Pleased to meet you."

Emma nodded. "Me, too."

Linda Enger, the owner of the only café in Dry Creek, was next. She was long and leggy and wore a denim skirt with a leather belt. Her flannel shirt was tucked into her waistband. She did not bother with a handshake but opened her arms and gave Emma a hug. "I've been wanting to meet you. I'm glad you're here on the ranch."

"Thank you," Emma said. She was pleased to meet someone who owned a café. If she decided to stay around here, maybe she could get a job with her. Not that now was the time to ask about that, Emma told herself.

Mary Baker was the one Emma instantly thought would be her friend. Shy and hesitant, the slender woman stood there twisting her hands and leaned over to Emma and whispered, "I should have worn my other dress."

"Don't worry," Emma said just as softly. "Bailey is loaning me this pretty blouse. Otherwise I'd have on a stretched-out pink sweatshirt with frayed cuffs."

Mary smiled and continued. "I always find something else to buy instead of clothes for myself."

"I know how that goes," Emma sympathized. "I'm hoping all of that doesn't need to matter here, though."

"It doesn't," a chorus of voices rang out, and Emma realized their conversation had been overheard.

"Wear what you have, eat all the chocolate you can and pray with your whole heart," Bailey announced. "That's our way."

Emma looked around and saw nothing but friendly faces. Mary moved over slightly and patted a space on the couch next to her so Emma sat down. She wondered if maybe she hadn't misjudged those church women in the past. Maybe they had felt as awkward giving out charity as she had felt receiving it.

Mrs. Hargrove read from the Bible about the woman at the well who met Jesus when she came to get water.

The fact that the woman was an outcast from the village and had to get water when no one else was around struck a chord with Emma, and she thought it did with Mary, too. They both took the small booklets Mrs. Hargrove gave them to explain the passage further.

Throughout the study, Emma was remembering the sweetness of her young days in church—before she knew what charity was—when her mother had taken her to Sunday school. Before Emma had time to relive all of those earlier memories, the Bible study had moved on to a time of prayer. She was hesitant at first to bring up anything personal, but Bailey asked if Emma would like them to pray for her and her coming baby.

"Thank you." Emma nodded. That was a safe request. The others prayed with love for her and her unborn child, and it made Emma feel good. Mary even slipped her hand into Emma's after the prayer and offered her the use of the crib she'd used with her sons when they were infants. Emma couldn't recall anyone praying for her before, and Mary had such a hopeful look on her face after she mentioned the crib that Emma wouldn't have refused the offer for anything. There was a difference, Emma told herself, between friendship and charity.

After that, Bailey beamed as she asked for guidance as she and Mark planned their wedding. "We don't want a lot of fuss, but we want it to be special. We're thinking a couple of months from now when there will be flowers in bloom. We're hoping we can have the ceremony at the ranch here. And, of course, you're all invited."

After Mary's kindness, Emma could only say, "If I can help in any way, let me know."

Bailey looked very pleased. "Thanks. I'll take you up on that."

Next, Mary asked for prayer for her and her boys. "My youngest boy is starting to have nightmares again. And the older two are worried."

"Are they concerned about Joe coming back—that's the name of the handyman you had, isn't it?" Linda asked.

Mary blushed. "That's him—Joseph O'Brien—but I think the boys want him to come back. They weren't afraid when he was there—especially after he told us about his PTSD and we worked on that. It's their father they are worried about coming back."

Emma put a comforting hand on Mary's shoulder. She knew how many hard feelings and violent tendencies could arise in a family—and how hard it was to talk about it with others.

Mary leaned into Emma a little and seemed comforted. "Their father was a mean man. No other words for it. I tried to stop him, but then he'd just beat on us all."

"And you want him back?" Emma asked in astonishment.

"I want to know where he is," Mary clarified.

"What brought this on?" Mrs. Hargrove asked as she shifted in the recliner where she sat and gazed thoughtfully at the other woman. "He's been gone for years."

Mary turned pink, and Emma realized the woman was as pretty as a china doll when she let go of the stiffness in her face.

"I thought we were doing fine, just me and the

boys," Mary said. "But the boys decided I should date and get married to someone so they'd have a proper father. I had to explain that I am still married to their father even though he abandoned us over three—almost four—years ago, and I don't even know where he is anymore."

Emma patted Mary's hand as she said, "I'm guessing they want you to marry this Mr. O'Brien."

Mary turned to face her. "I couldn't do that." Her face went deep red, and she sputtered. "I'd never. I mean, I'm a married woman."

"Whose husband has been gone for not months but years," Emma said. "And whose husband is probably married up to someone else by now."

Emma didn't realize what she'd said until the words hung out there with no place to land. She gently took her hand back from Mary's grip. "I'm sorry. I didn't mean—I mean, not many men actually fake a wedding."

Emma winced. That was worse. Bailey wasn't even looking at her, and Linda Enger had raised her eyebrows.

"I need to stop right now, don't I?" Emma said looking at the floor. "I forgot to mention I'm one of those *open mouth, insert foot* kind of people. That's me."

It was silent for a moment.

"I've had a couple of those incidents myself," Linda Enger finally said supportively. "So embarrassing."

Mary giggled. "Me, too."

"You?" The surprise of that confession made Emma lift her head to look at the shy woman. "I can't believe you make any awkward statements."

"Sometimes she does it on purpose," Bailey added

with a smile. She seemed to have regained her composure. "Not to be mean, of course. To be amusing. She's not as quiet as she seems."

"It started with my boys," Mary admitted. "They used to get into too many fights. Mr. O'Brien started teaching them to play little practical jokes with each other instead—nothing mean, just something unexpected, like when Billy was supposed to gather the eggs and one of the other boys went out and did it first so Billy came in worried about not finding any eggs and saying the chickens must be dying." Mary grinned. "It's been much better at our house with those kinds of things, and I'm trying to learn to joke some myself. I'm not very good at it yet, but I try."

"Bless that man," Mrs. Hargrove said.

A chorus of *Amens* followed.

Finally, Mary started slowly talking again. "The boys asking for a father might have been Mr. O'Brien's fault. This was before the lessons on joking. He started to write to the boys. He's been in that veterans' program for his PTSD over in Idaho. He'd send each one a letter every week. They are thrilled. They get them on Thursdays and sleep with them under their pillows until the next one comes."

"Your Mr. O'Brien shows some kindness," Linda said approvingly.

"At first, I didn't think it was a good idea," Mary continued. "The boys cared too much about those letters. I know they've never even gotten a postcard from anyone else, but…" Mary stared off into space and then brought herself back. "The thing is they are good letters. Usually, he encourages them to do well in school and obey me—that kind of thing."

"No harm in that," Emma interjected, trying to be supportive. She owed Mary for helping her past her awkward moment.

Bailey cleared her throat, and when Emma looked over, the other woman smiled right at her and added, "No harm in anything that is said here, either. We're friends. Don't be afraid of speaking up."

Emma swallowed. "I won't. Thank you."

Mary put her hand out to Emma again and continued. "I guess one of the boys—probably Billy—wrote and said they wanted a father. Mr. O'Brien is the one that suggested I start to date again. He even offered to guide the boys in how to help me find a good man to marry."

Mary sounded exhausted. Emma guessed the other woman wasn't used to sharing this much about herself and her boys.

"I have no idea how to even find my husband—I mean the one I have," Mary admitted, sounding discouraged. "I've been praying, but nothing happens. I wonder sometimes if he came down with amnesia or something."

"I knew him well, and I doubt that," Mrs. Hargrove said firmly. "I believe God can redeem any man, but your husband would be a challenge."

"I'm sure Gabe Rosen knows how to find him," Emma said, remembering the conversation with him from the previous night. She wanted to do something nice for Mary, and this might be it. "He's going to locate my father for me. What's one more person to look for?"

"Oh," Mary gasped. "Do you think he could find him?"

"We can certainly ask him," Bailey said, sounding encouraging. "Gabe is good at what he does. And he pays for some kind of service that gives him more information and contacts to locate people than others would have. It might not be that hard with all he has to help him. Have you ever asked the sheriff's department to help?"

"The deputy sheriff, Carl Wall, wrote a report," Mary said. "But…at first, one of the sheriffs in Helena suggested I might have murdered him and was trying to cover it up. I was terrified. They came and looked all over our place. Of course, they didn't find anything. But I stopped calling to ask if they had any progress on finding him."

"Goodness," Mrs. Hargrove said. "I hope Carl told the office in Helena that it was ridiculous to think you could have killed that man. He was three times your size!"

"He did tell them," Mary said, "but they were checking for poison. Of course, we don't have anything like that at our place because of the boys. I was glad for that."

They were all silent for a minute. Emma didn't think the other women had known this, either.

"It would solve your problems if you found him," Linda said. "No one could accuse you of anything, then. And you could ask him to officially divorce you. If he'd wanted to be married, he would be back by now."

"It would be an answer to prayer just to know." Mary squeezed the hand Emma held. "It would change my life if I didn't feel I was in limbo waiting for either him or the sheriffs to come back."

The women spent some minutes in prayer, and when Emma opened her eyes after that, she saw Rosie and Tommy standing in the doorway looking excited.

"How have you two been doing?" Emma asked the children as she started to stand up. She'd forgotten how big with child she was, though, and Mary had to help her.

"Sorry about that," Emma said when she was upright. "It's getting more difficult to get out of a soft chair like this."

"I know how that goes," Mary said. "After three babies, I always said that when I got so big I just couldn't get up it was a sign that it wouldn't be too long until the baby decided to come."

"Speaking of that baby," Bailey said as she stood as well, "are you set for everything? Did that doctor's appointment yesterday tell you what you needed to know?"

Emma nodded, and the women all started gathering up their purses and coats.

"Mama," Rosie called from the doorway, "we need to pass the cookies."

"Oh, I forgot," Bailey said as she looked around. "Five more minutes. Rosie and Tommy have been so well behaved, and they want to pass the cookies for us. I have the trays all set so it won't take long."

Emma remained standing, as did Mary.

"We never did ask," Emma whispered to Mary when everyone else's attention was on the cookies. "I know I haven't known you long, and it's not my business—"

"Oh, no," Mary protested. "I feel we're already friends. You can ask anything."

Emma ducked her head, more pleased than she

wanted to show. "Okay, then. Do you want to get married again if you're free to? I mean have you met someone?"

"Not really," Mary said a little hesitantly. She was silent for a few minutes. "There are some nice men around, though—" Mary sounded like she didn't want to name anyone, but then she looked up just as heavy footsteps could be heard coming from the kitchen. Emma's eyes followed to where Mary's gaze went, and she saw Joshua and, of course, Mark. They were each exiting the kitchen carrying a plate of cookies and following Rosie and Tommy. Joshua in particular was smiling. It made her feel better just to see him.

"Like Joshua there," Mary said softly, and Emma wondered if she'd said the name aloud. But Mary was looking at him on her own, her voice rich with some emotion that hadn't been there before.

Emma had to think to catch up. "Joshua what?"

"He's nice," Mary said, keeping her voice low so no one else could hear. Her eyes were dancing. "And good with children. Maybe not as exciting as a woman would want, but he's steady."

"That's not true," Emma protested in spite of all her common sense. "He's plenty exciting. Why—"

Mary just stood there and grinned at her.

"You—" Emma was almost speechless. "I—"

"I thought I detected a spark," Mary said serenely, her eyes full of mischief.

Emma's eyes narrowed as she looked at the other woman.

"Was that one of your jokes?" Emma asked indignantly and then, a moment later, couldn't help the giggles that followed. She'd never had a sister or a girlfriend before to tease her about men. "Just for that, I'm going to help those boys of yours find a man you can't resist."

"Not until I'm divorced, you won't," Mary said, all of the lightness gone from her voice. "I want them to know marriage is a bond not to be made lightly and not to be undone easily."

By the time Mary finished talking, all four plates of cookies had been offered in their direction. Emma took a chocolate sandwich cookie dipped in deep chocolate. Mary settled for a small piece of shortbread. They ate standing up.

Emma was content to stay there and enjoy her new-found friendship.

"You two seem to be having a good time," Joshua observed to the women as the pint-size servers decided to sit down and help themselves to the extra cookies.

"We were just talking," Emma said, keeping her voice bland.

Mary snorted and couldn't hold back her laughter.

That made Emma giggle. Joshua beamed at them both and moved away to keep passing his plate of cookies.

Emma watched Joshua bow when he came to Rosie and Tommy. He offered both children some cookies with proper butler grace. Mary was right about that man, Emma thought, as the other women got ready to leave. He was good with children. As to exciting, well—she best not be thinking about that, or Mary would get her going again.

The women went to get their coats, and Tommy went to the rack by the door and pulled down the coat he'd worn, too. He made a disgusted face, but he put it on.

"Oh," Mrs. Hargrove hurried over. "I was hoping Tommy would have some time to talk about the pictures in the book."

Tommy nodded, and his face beamed. "Pictures."

Emma knew Mrs. Hargrove had mentioned that Tommy was interested in the children's Bible that had so many pictures in it.

But he was happily following Mrs. Hargrove.

"Lord, help us both," Emma whispered the prayer as she watched her brother head out. With the women all talking to God this afternoon like He was listening to them, Emma hoped that He could hear her concerns for Tommy. "Give my brother ears to hear," she added.

There was not time to pray more so she let her heart relax. They were among friends. And Joshua was here.

"I was wondering," he said as he stood there. "I don't know your middle name."

"Will you need it for the doctor?" she asked anxiously. "It's Ann—Emma Ann Smitt. That's my legal name."

Joshua nodded. "And what's your favorite color?"

Emma realized he must be as worried as she was about all the forms related to the hospital. "I don't think the hospital rooms come in many different colors."

"But if they did?" he persisted.

"Something pastel, I suppose," Emma answered. "I like a soothing room to sleep in."

"Would lilac work?" he asked.

"That's always been a special color to me," she responded with a smile. "But I think the hospital goes more toward white and beige. Maybe light gray."

Joshua nodded and didn't say anything more. She

was touched that he was a little stressed about all of this, though. It was nice to have someone go through it all with her. Mary was right; Joshua was a nice man.

Chapter Ten

Joshua ate a couple of coconut cookies as he sat in Bailey's living room and watched the women who lived elsewhere leave. The afternoon was growing late. It would be dark in a couple more hours. And he couldn't be happier. He could tell by the way Emma had spoken with Mary that they were on the way to becoming friends. He had the impression that Emma hadn't had many friends in her life, and he hoped that would make her more willing to stay here even after the baby was born.

As the others left, he had watched Mrs. Hargrove pull a big book off the coffee table and invite Tommy over to her chair.

"She's explaining about Jesus," Emma whispered to Joshua as she bent down close to where he was sitting. She'd already told him she wanted to stand for a bit, but she must have changed her mind. He suspected it was hard for her to be comfortable anywhere.

"Let me get you a chair," he said as he stood. "Here. You can have my place."

Emma shook her head. "I can't get up out of the soft chairs."

"Oh, that's right." Joshua changed his direction and brought over a straight-backed chair.

Emma sat down and watched Tommy for some time. "I know it's important, and I hope he'll be able to understand," she finally said as she turned to Joshua.

He'd been watching along with her and could tell she was tense.

"Tommy's smart," Joshua assured her. He could hear the steady murmur of Mrs. Hargrove's voice. She had taught hundreds of Dry Creek children about God. Surely, she knew all of the words.

"I know, but Tommy sees things different," Emma replied. "He doesn't always go straight at an idea. He needs to make it fit in his head right."

Joshua nodded. That's what he thought, too.

Maybe Tommy sensed them watching him, because he looked up and sent a pleading look right in Joshua's direction.

"He's confused," Emma said. "Maybe you can rescue him. We can try another day."

Joshua walked over and squatted down beside Tommy.

"Maybe you can help us, Joshua," Mrs. Hargrove said. "Tommy wants to know more about who God is. I know that, but I can't find the words to make myself clear."

Joshua smiled. It was like the older woman to place the blame on herself and not Tommy. The boy seemed to be sensitive about that. And then Joshua had an idea.

"Jesus has big shoulders," Joshua said and repeated it with a hand gesture of width. "Big shoulders."

"Put Tommy's bad?" the boy asked in excitement, obviously remembering their previous conversations.

"That's right," Joshua said encouragingly. "He takes all of the Tommy bad and puts it on his shoulders. No more bad for Tommy. All Tommy needs to do is say he is sorry for his bad and ask Jesus to help him do good."

Tommy nodded. "No bad Tommy."

"All good with Jesus," Joshua assured him.

"You're getting there," Mrs. Hargrove said in a voice warm with approval. "Now, how do we explain about the new life he'll have?"

Joshua stood up and walked over to where he'd hung his coat. It wasn't his warmest coat and was really more of a jacket than a long coat. It was black denim with a quilted lining. He brought it back with him.

"Do you like the coat you have?" Joshua asked the boy.

Tommy shook his head vigorously. "Stinks. Bad."

Joshua solemnly took off Tommy's coat. "Old stink gone for Tommy. Old life gone."

Joshua dramatically tossed the old coat into the corner of the living room. Then he put his coat on the wide-eyed boy. "New life for Tommy with Jesus. No more bad. No more stink."

"Jesus make Tommy good," the boy said, tears running down his face. "No more bad."

"That's right," Mrs. Hargrove said as she gave Tommy a hug. "That's exactly right."

Joshua looked over and saw the tears streaming down Emma's face. He had a few tears sliding down his cheeks, too.

"Jesus always with Tommy," Joshua added.

"Jesus with Emma, too?" Tommy asked as his eyes went to his sister.

Joshua looked at Emma again. Tears were still streaming down her face, but she smiled at Joshua and nodded.

"Yes, Jesus with Emma, too," Joshua said and lifted his heart in gratitude. *Thank You, Lord, for Your mercies to us.* For the first time, he had to admit there was such a thing as walking-on-water faith. God was bigger than he'd thought. God didn't need Joshua to make any plans. He knew what needed to happen.

Joshua felt God touch his soul, and he knew he could trust Him in return.

And looking at the joy on Emma's face, he knew she felt God's hand, too. These were hallelujah days.

The next two days went by slowly for Emma. She read and reread the pamphlet from the Bible study and marveled over what she was learning about God. But for the rest of the time she felt like a bloated elephant with particularly large ankles. She could no longer even waddle at a steady pace.

Bailey had brought over a whole stack of bridal magazines, and Emma sat in bed and thumbed through them. She had a notebook with her and wrote down questions and notes for Bailey to consider. She concentrated on outdoor ceremonies and flowers. Weddings, she'd stop to sigh periodically, were such lovely events, and she wanted to do what she could to make Bailey's perfect.

The fake one Emma had had with Junior had been little more than a bare-bones minister's office event, not even with a real minister. Just thinking about it left a bad taste in her mouth. If she ever got married again, she'd have fresh flowers all over the place. And she'd make sure the minister was real.

By the third day, Emma couldn't stay still. Everything annoyed her—the wrinkles in her sheets, the snorts from that bird in the other part of the bunkhouse and the slightly crooked way the curtains hung. In the middle of the morning, she walked over to Bailey's house and announced she was making Swedish pancakes for everyone for the noon meal, despite Bailey's protests that sandwiches were fine.

"How many sandwiches have we eaten in the past week?" Emma demanded to know.

"Ten," Rosie complained from the corner of the table where she sat. "We don't even have any of the good bread left. I think we're having crackers now—without peanut butter. And no jam."

"But we're fine," Bailey responded as she shook her head at her daughter. "Emma doesn't need to wait on us."

"I'm tired of lying in bed," Emma declared as she pulled an apron out of the drawer by the sink and then threw it across the kitchen when it was apparent the ties would not go all of the way around her. "And even more tired of feeling like an elephant!"

Emma had raised her voice, and Rosie stared at her with eyes wide open in surprise.

"You're looking fine," Bailey insisted.

Emma protested. "An old elephant who can barely move enough to keep up with the rest of the circus!"

"Are we going to go see a circus?" Rosie asked in rising excitement as she stood up from her chair. "I've never been to a circus. They have peanuts there. We could have peanuts for dinner."

"Not now," Bailey said as she bent down and whispered something in Rosie's ear which made the girl tear out of the house, barely stopping to get her coat.

Bailey turned to look at Emma cautiously.

"I'm not a danger to anyone," she grumbled as she started to crack eggs. "And I love Swedish pancakes. I don't suppose you have any kind of berry syrup?"

"I think we have some bottles of blueberry syrup," Bailey answered carefully. "Or maybe it's boysenberry. I'm not sure."

"Boysenberry would work well," Emma said as she reached up to pull down a measuring cup. "I think to be Swedish it's supposed to be lingonberry, but who's even heard of that?"

"I went to a Swedish church some when I was in Los Angeles, and they made Swedish pancakes," Bailey said in a soothing voice. "I think it was a Covenant church of some sort. They used lingonberry syrup."

"Good for them." By this time, Emma had the flour measured into a bowl separate from the eggs. "I'll need a frying pan, too." She looked at Bailey again. "Are you Swedish?"

Bailey shook her head. "I don't know, but I doubt it. I spent my first few years in foster homes until I was adopted by a family in Dry Creek. Mark also grew up in foster care. We met when we were both about Tommy's age."

"I didn't know that," Emma said as she stopped stirring. "So neither one of you had real families—I mean, well, you know what I mean."

"We made our own families," Bailey said. "It's not about blood ties with us; it's about the heart."

"That's—" Emma started to say something when suddenly all of her energy was gone, and she couldn't quite remember what she meant to say. *Incredible*, maybe that was it. Or was it *astonishing*?

Just then the kitchen door was flung open, and Joshua came racing inside. Emma noticed he hadn't stopped to scrape the mud off of his boots. But that probably didn't matter because he had some light purple stuff on his shirt and more of it on his pant legs. It looked like lilac paint, but that made no sense. The only building out that way was the barn. She doubted the cows wanted lilac stalls.

"Are you all right?" Joshua demanded as he stopped right next to Emma and put his arms out. "Rosie said there was trouble."

"Ah, Rosie," Emma said, feeling even more woozy. She decided that since Joshua had his arms right there and they were so handy, she would lean into him a little. Before she knew it, he had her wrapped up tight in his arms, and he was leading her to one of the kitchen chairs.

"Don't you fall," he whispered softly as he helped her waddle to the chair. Once there, he settled her and squatted down to look at her. "We need to take care of little 'Night, night'."

Emma blinked and swallowed. "'Night, night'."

That was so sweet, she thought.

"Now, what's wrong?" he asked in concern.

She didn't know what he meant. Everything was fine. Then she looked deep into his eyes. He had the nicest eyes—which, for some reason, made her burst into tears and wail just like she was Rosie's age. "I wanted Swedish pancakes."

By this time, Rosie had crowded close and patted Emma on the cheek. "With some berry syrup," the girl reminded her before looking up at Joshua. "Doesn't that sound good?"

"It does," Joshua admitted cautiously as he glanced over at the cupboard counter. "Do you want me to finish them up?"

Emma nodded. "Please."

"I'll help," Bailey offered.

"I've got it." Joshua went over and picked up the apron Emma had tossed earlier. He tied it around his waist where it fit nicely, she noted in despair. She was a blimp.

Then he turned to Bailey and said, "You go keep Emma company."

Bailey walked over and gave Emma a hug.

"Thanks," Emma whispered. "I'm a mess."

"You're expecting is what you are," Bailey said firmly. "Carrying a baby is a blessing. But we can't pretend it doesn't affect us."

By then Joshua was washing his hands at the sink.

Emma had to admit she enjoyed sitting in the chair watching Joshua finish the pancake batter and answering a question from him now and then on how to go on. It felt good to let her responsibilities just go by, like she was sitting on the beach and not at the kitchen table.

Soon enough little Rosie came, and she and Tommy set the table with plates and silverware. Joshua was making progress with the pancakes, and she noticed he'd pulled a syrup bottle from someplace. Bailey had been called away to tend to Lilly, but then she brought the baby back and sat down at the table again.

"I still feel like I have a watermelon inside me," Emma said, feeling a bit of self-pity. Her words made Rosie giggle, though, and that set Tommy off until finally Emma shrugged her shoulders and gave up her feelings to giggle with them.

Maybe it was all of the giggling, but when Rosie went over to where Bailey sat with Lilly, Emma could hear the baby gurgle. Rosie set the glass she held down on the table and bent over to peer more closely at Lilly.

Emma wondered if she should get up and make sure Rosie kept her distance from the baby. After all, the girl hadn't seemed to be impressed with her sibling.

But then Rosie straightened and looked up at her mother with the sweetest look on her face.

"The baby smiled at me," Rosie said in awe. "Me. She smiled at me."

"Of course," Bailey said. "You're her big sister. You're going to help her learn how to walk and maybe even show her how to tie her first pair of shoes. You'll take her on her first wagon ride and make sure she knows to stay close to the house and not get near the cows."

"I'll be her big sister," Rosie repeated proudly.

The kitchen door opened then, and Mark stepped inside. Rosie ran to him and announced, "I get to be the baby's big sister!"

Mark bent down and scooped the girl up. "You'll be a great one!"

"And you'll be the baby's daddy, too?" Rosie asked, sounding a little uncertain. "She'll need a daddy. I'll share."

"It'll be my pleasure," Mark said as he carried Rosie a few steps and then bent down with her in his arms so he could kiss Bailey.

"Don't forget to kiss the baby," Rosie said.

Mark obliged.

Emma was almost in tears again. She needed to stop these hormone rushes. Maybe she needed a teddy bear to hug. Fortunately, Joshua and Tommy were both facing the stove and couldn't see her falling apart. People saw these kinds of scenes with children all the time. She didn't need to water up every time Rosie showed her heart to the world.

"Time for pancakes," Joshua announced, and he and Tommy both brought platters of golden brown Swedish pancakes to the table. Joshua had even fried sausage links to go with them.

"That smells delicious," Mark said and just like that the conversation shifted from daddy kisses to instructions on how to eat pancakes without getting one's fingers sticky.

The Swedish pancakes were thin and tasted wonderful with the boysenberry syrup. Emma ate her fill and was soon ready to go back to her perch on the bed. Maybe Bailey would come over this afternoon, she told herself, and they'd talk about wedding fantasies. Emma had seen a beautiful picture of a wedding setup on a ranch somewhere using lilacs. Emma could almost smell the blossoms in the picture. Maybe Bailey would like to use lilacs if they could find any close by. She knew they grew in Montana. She'd have to ask her. She lay back on her bed and closed her eyes. She felt a tiny twinge and wondered if it was a contraction. No, she thought as she lay there. It couldn't be.

Chapter Eleven

The next morning was bright, but not warm. Joshua figured it was a good day to drive to Miles City, though, since Emma was taking another nap and Tommy was staying with Max and Cupid. Yesterday, he and Mark had finished painting two bedrooms, the living room and kitchen in the Durham house, and he needed to buy a few things. First, he'd buy white sheets and purple towels for Emma's room and then some large sections of corkboard to go on the yellow walls in Tommy's room. The boy would have plenty of room to tack up his pictures.

Joshua didn't want to ruin any of the surprise for either one of them by letting anyone know what he was doing.

Of course, the other reason for making the drive was to be alone so he could think. Since the Swedish pancakes, when Emma had shown her anxieties so clearly, he had been aware that he needed, and wanted, to show more of his emotions to her. That scared him because he had slowly realized over the past few days that he wasn't going to ever get his smooth-talking

ways back. He would not be able to make his failings
sound charming. If he wanted Emma to know him, he
was going to have to do it the old-fashioned way. He
was going to have to take it on the chin and lay everything right out there for her. He'd rather walk through
a bed of hot coals than have her know his failures. But
he had to do it because he had to trust Emma with his
heart if they were going to have a future. He had to go
all the way back in his life to when he trusted his father and shouldn't have. Only this time, it was Emma
he needed to trust, and she needed to feel the same
way about him.

On the drive in to Miles City, he decided he should
take Mark's advice and buy Emma a box of candy just
to prime the conversational pump. Then he realized that, given her comments about feeling like an elephant, that it might not be a sound strategy. Instead,
before going home, he swung by a florist and bought
her a dozen red roses. He'd wanted lilacs, but the florist assured him they never had that flower for sale. At
least the roses would give him some time if he found
he was speechless.

"Lord, help me to do this right," he prayed. He'd already botched that kiss the bird talked him into. One
thing he knew for sure, he wasn't going to have his
heart-to-heart anywhere near Cupid.

Everything was quiet when he pulled into the driveway of the Rosen Ranch. He thought Emma would
be in the bunkhouse, but he left the roses on the seat
of his pickup and walked inside the building only to
find Tommy and Max trying to teach Cupid how to
say something.

"Emma here?" he asked.

They both shook their heads, and Max said, "Main house."

Joshua went back to the pickup and grabbed the bouquet of roses in one hand. He stretched the other hand under the seat and pulled out that cigar box. He had a large brown paper bag on the seat, and he slipped the cigar box into it. He was going to have to tell Emma everything, but he didn't want anyone coming to see what he had in the cigar box.

He found her sitting at the table in the kitchen, looking down at a recipe book. She had her chestnut hair pulled back into a ponytail, and she was wearing her old pink sweatshirt over her denim jeans. She was frowning slightly at the book and seemed to be weighing some decision.

"Looking for lunch?" he asked as he walked into the kitchen with the paper bag in one hand and the roses behind his back in the other hand.

She glanced up and smiled. "Rosie's tired of sandwiches."

"She told me she loved my sandwiches," Joshua protested.

"She's got a tender heart," Emma said. "And she's afraid that if she complains, you'll open that jar of stewed tomatoes and dish her up those or maybe dig out that can of sardines that she hid at the back of the cupboard. She thinks they're both slimy."

"Who is she kidding?" Joshua protested. "She loves to imagine disaster food."

"Maybe," Emma said. "But she doesn't want to actually have to eat it."

Joshua realized he hadn't even thought to get groceries, something he never would do. Maybe Rosie was right to worry, but he couldn't think about that now.

"Do you have a minute to talk?" Joshua asked as he stepped closer.

"Sure," she said. "I've got lots of time. I was just tired of lying down. I was getting these little cramps."

"It's not the baby?" Joshua asked, searching her face for any sign of distress.

"No," she assured him. "I probably just need a little exercise."

"I could come back later," Joshua said.

By this time, he realized that by him turning this way and that Emma had likely seen the roses. He noticed a spark of interest in her eyes.

"I wanted to get to know you better," Joshua said as he brought the roses out from behind his back and presented them to her.

Emma chuckled as she gathered the flowers to her and sniffed them. "You've seen me at my worst. I'm not sure there's a lot more to know."

"It's not so much you as it is me," Joshua said as he set the paper bag on the table and pulled out the cigar box setting it down close to Emma. "I want you to know me, too."

The cigar box was closed, but he could see she was already interested.

Joshua sat down and put his hand on the box. "It is bad."

"Okay," she said. "Tell me your worst. No, I take that back. It's probably just jaywalking, and that would be depressing."

"Oh, it's much worse than jaywalking," Joshua assured her. "I suppose it all started when I was growing up. As I told you, I was six years old when my sister died, and child services said I couldn't stay with my parents. My relatives set up this system where I went from house to house. Mostly relatives, but some of them pretty distant. A few weeks here. A few months there. Usually I went wherever farm work was needed. I was good at that. But no place really felt like home to me."

She murmured something sounding sympathetic, but he had to keep going.

"I got into trouble in my teen years and landed in a juvenile detention place for a year," he added. "Learned more than I needed to know there and ended up with this." Joshua opened the cigar box. Hundred-dollar bills spilled out.

"Oh, my," Emma said, shock in her voice. "Did you rob a bank?"

Joshua shook his head. "No, it was poker."

"The card game?" she asked.

"Yes," Joshua nodded. "I plan to give it to charity."

"Did you cheat?" she asked, sounding a little puzzled.

"No," Joshua answered. "But I took advantage of people, talking them into playing when they couldn't afford to lose and distracting them with some nonsense so they couldn't play well."

"That doesn't sound like you," Emma said.

"I know," Joshua said and gave a sigh. She might as well know all of it. "I can't sweet-talk my way out of a paper bag anymore. I don't mind so much about not being able to play poker. But there was a day when I could be sitting here with you, and I would have you grinning ear to ear with some nonsense."

"So, you used the same fast talking to get along better with people?" she asked.

Joshua nodded. "I could get along with anyone. Mr. Congeniality—that was me. It didn't matter what the truth of the matter really was, I'd dress things up until they sounded great." He paused. "Sort of like Junior did when he told you those earrings were diamonds."

He saw a painful expression flit across Emma's face. It was like she tasted something sour.

"The problem is that I didn't trust anyone," Joshua continued. "I didn't want to rely on them, and I didn't want them to rely on me. I didn't want them to even know me.

"I won't blame you if you don't want to be..." Joshua almost mentioned marrying him, but it didn't seem the best moment for that "...have much to do with me."

Emma's face softened and she reached over to pat his hand. "It's not that. From what you told me about your sister, you learned early not to trust anyone. And I can understand why you used to sweet-talk people. You had to as a child or you'd never have a place to stay. But it's different now that you're on the ranch here with Mark and Bailey. They see you as family. You've got a home here. You don't need to be glib with anyone. You belong. You can let people know you."

"Oh." Joshua sat back in his chair. He felt like his emotions had been laid bare. It was true he had always been anxious as a child. Lots of people liked him a little, but no one loved him. He couldn't count on anyone. He'd never thought of that. Maybe it wasn't God yanking his glib tongue away from him as much as it was God saying he didn't need it any longer. He could trust people. Emma was right when she said he had a home.

"How did you know?" Joshua asked. No one else had taken the time to see his insecurity, his lack of trust.

Emma started to answer, but then she gasped. The pain was back in her face. "I think it's time."

"Baby time?" Joshua asked his heart starting to pound. *Lord, help us here.*

"I think so," Emma nodded.

"Bailey," Joshua yelled. "Mark."

Everyone rushed into the kitchen, alarm on all of their faces.

"It's time," Joshua said. "Emma's baby is coming."

"We'll want to take her in the van," Bailey said as she raced over to where the vehicle keys hung by the refrigerator.

Joshua stood up and hovered over Emma. "Can you stand up with my help?"

"Mrs. Hargrove can stay here with Lilly," Mark said as he glanced over at the older woman. "Will that work?"

She nodded.

"Rosie and Tommy can stay with you, too," Mark said as he was leaving the kitchen. "I'll get the van."

"Me go," Tommy said stubbornly as he walked over and stood by Joshua. "Tommy go. Sister."

Emma gave another gasp as she tried to rise, and Joshua decided they'd all go. Tommy had as much right as anyone. And if the boy went, then Rosie would have to go. He could already hear the van starting up.

"Let's go," Joshua said as he stuffed the cigar box back into the bag and picked it up. They might need the cash tonight. "Coats, everyone."

A few minutes later the van was heading down the

gravel road outside the Rosen Ranch property at a high speed. Mark was driving. Bailey was in the front passenger seat, looking back at Emma who was in the middle passenger seat with Joshua in the same row. Tommy and Rosie were huddled silently in the back row.

"Breathe, now, breathe," Joshua said as Emma squeezed his hand until she stopped his circulation. He didn't care. She was scared.

"I called ahead to the number on your instruction sheet," Joshua assured her as he put his free arm around her.

"Are we there yet?" Emma asked after five minutes.

"Not yet," Joshua said. "We're going as fast as the stork can go."

She smiled and rolled her eyes. "Don't you—" She gasped again and didn't complete her thought.

Joshua searched for something reassuring to say. Finally, all he could muster was "Hang in there. We love you."

That made her smile, but he was worried it threw the rhythm of her breathing off. "Now take a breath." He waited a beat. "And another one."

"Don't keep nagging," Emma managed to say between breaths.

About then they pulled into the medical clinic. A couple of orderlies stood waiting and quickly moved her into a wheelchair. Emma had filled out her information so she was immediately carried away to the small maternity area.

Several hours later, Joshua and the others were still huddled together in the large waiting room with its rows of plastic chairs. With his back to the door Mark was holding a sleeping Rosie on his lap, and Bailey was cuddled in next to him. Facing them and the door, Joshua sat the paper bag at his feet and Tommy beside him. The windows in the room looked out over the early spring day. Snow was almost gone from the ground, but no new grass was coming up yet. Everything was quiet. It was late afternoon.

Joshua took a minute to go to the billing department in the clinic.

By the time he got back, Rosie was fussing her way awake. Tommy watched the girl carefully as she blinked a few times and then put her hand on Mark's shoulder possessively. "Daddy. My daddy."

Joshua heard Tommy start to squirm. He had a frown on his face as he watched Rosie. It wasn't long before he was looking up at Joshua.

"Rosie daddy?" he asked Joshua as he pointed at Mark.

"That's right," Joshua said. "That's her daddy, now."

Tommy was silent then, and Joshua almost missed it as Tommy slid a little closer to him.

"Tommy daddy?" the boy asked softly as he pointed at Joshua.

"Oh," Joshua said. Tommy's gaze was full of a shy eagerness that touched Joshua's heart. "I hope so."

He didn't know how he could promise anything more to the boy. He loved Tommy, but Emma was the boy's guardian, and it was not really Joshua's choice. He loved Emma, too, but whether she returned any of his feelings he didn't know.

Joshua didn't get any more words out, and Tommy finally looked away in resignation.

Joshua bit back a bitter sound. Then he looked at

Tommy's eyes again and opened his arms. He'd deal with the consequences later. "I'll be your daddy."

Tommy scrambled into Joshua's lap as fast as he could and leaned back on Joshua's shoulder looking content. "Tommy daddy."

Joshua held him closer, not daring to look over at Mark and Bailey. They were adults and would know he had overstepped his place.

"Every boy needs a daddy," Mark said softly, and Joshua looked up at the other man and Bailey. Neither one of them looked like Joshua should have said anything different than he had.

It was full dark before a doctor came out to tell them that Emma had given birth to a baby boy. "She's exhausted," the doctor added. "She asked to just go to sleep tonight. I suggest someone check back in with us in the morning."

"She's all right?" Joshua asked the doctor.

The man smiled and said, "Right as can be."

Joshua knew he had to stay, but he suggested Mark and Bailey take the two children home.

"But you won't be able to sleep," Bailey protested. "Those chairs aren't comfortable."

"I don't need to sleep," he answered.

"Call us in the morning," Mark said and gave Joshua's arm a squeeze. "I know how it is."

Joshua sat there and watched the night slowly turn gray and then, hours later, turn darker. He marveled at the words Emma had spoken to him before her pains started. How did she know he'd been searching for a home for a long time? The only thing she got wrong was that it wasn't living at the Rosen Ranch that had given him a home, it was having Emma and Tommy with him that made that bunkhouse an anchor to him.

And now there was a baby boy, too. He figured he wouldn't have been able to sleep tonight even if there was a feather bed in the waiting room. He was a man with too much joy inside him to sleep. He could not wait for the sun to rise.

Emma woke up before dark had broken. The curtains in the clinic room were only partially closed and it was gray outside. It was quiet everywhere, and the clock beside her bed declared it was five in the morning. Her baby was in the nursery down the hall, and Emma was happy. They'd brought the baby down to nurse several hours ago. She wished she had been feeling well enough last night to ask Joshua to come back and meet the little boy, but maybe he would come later this morning after his chores.

Everything had shifted in her mind in the last few days, and then yesterday she had wondered if Joshua was working up his nerve to propose marriage to her. It made her heart warm just thinking about that. She felt he knew her and cared for her. And he seemed to understand her. She was not a woman who wanted to be weak and require someone to take care of her. The example of her mother's life haunted her. A woman could give up too much to a man who wanted to smother and dominate her—and make her so helpless she needed charity.

She saw a figure out of the corner of her eyes and turned to greet the nurse. But no nurse had curly brown hair and a height that reached taller than any of the staff she'd met so far.

"Joshua?" she whispered.

The figure stepped closer, and she knew it was him. He was wearing a surgical gown, but he even had that paper bag with him.

"They let me come in if I suited up," he whispered.

"But how did you get here so soon?" she asked. "You can't have finished your chores."

"I stayed overnight in the waiting room," he said. "And Mark will take care of everything on the ranch."

"Oh." She had not expected anyone to stay behind.

"I promised I wouldn't take too much time," Joshua said as he stepped closer and bent down to kiss her on the forehead. "But I wanted you to know I'm here."

Emma smiled. "That's nice."

"I hope to always be here for you wherever life leads," Joshua added in a whisper. "I don't want you to worry about making any decisions, but I wanted you to know I love you and, when you're back on the ranch, I plan to propose to you."

"Oh," Emma said, sitting up in her bed.

"I don't want you to think about it now," Joshua said hurriedly. "You've got plenty of time to decide. I just wanted you to know I'm here."

Emma almost told him that she didn't need any time to decide. She had realized when she was talking to him when her pains started that she trusted him. He knew her. Even more than Junior had. Her heart was racing. She thought she loved him. She didn't care if she'd made her decision quickly. It was right.

But then he lifted up that paper bag and put it beside her in the bed. "This is for you."

"Your poker money?" Emma asked with a little frown. "I can't take that."

"Sure you can," he said. "I want to give it to you."

"But you said it was for charity," Emma protested. Something was very wrong here.

"It is charity for you," Joshua said.

All of the hope drained out of Emma's heart. She knew he meant well, but he must not know her after all. How many times had she said she didn't take charity? How many times had he not paid attention? "No, thank you."

"But—" Joshua started to protest.

Emma turned so her back was toward him. "I'm tired."

She would have to see about going back to her mountain as soon as she and the baby were able to make the trip. She would rather be alone than be trapped with a man who didn't know her when she'd told him how important things like this were to her. She knew her mother would agree with her decision.

"I'll leave the box with you," Joshua said softly. "You can think about who you want to give it to."

Emma turned around. "What?"

"I thought you would like to give it to charity," Joshua said calmly. "It has to go to charity, but whichever ones you want are fine. Or even just people."

Joshua pulled the cigar box out of the paper bag and laid it on the bed beside her.

"You want me to give the money away?" Emma asked, needing to be sure. "To someone else?"

"Of course," Joshua said. "I know you don't like to receive charity. But I thought maybe you'd like to give it to others."

He opened the box. "It's quite a lot."

"Oh," Emma said feeling excited. He did know her.

And he was right. She would love to give charity to others. Not that she would ever make anyone feel self-conscious about taking it. But there were so many people who could use some help.

Emma felt around the edge of her pillow and found her grandmother's handkerchief. She had held that throughout the birth of her baby last night. Now she laid the handkerchief across the money in the box. "My mother and grandmother would be so proud if we could give this money to people who needed it. It would make up for a lot that they went through. I'll give it in their memory."

Emma stopped and looked up at Joshua. "You have no idea what this means to me."

"I think I do," Joshua said, with a big smile on his face.

"I thought the cigar box money was to pay my bill here," she said. "You're sure you don't want me to use it for that?"

Joshua shook his head. "I know that's not the right thing for you or for that money, either—that money needs to help others. No, I paid a deposit on your bill out of my bank account last night. After that, we'll be able to set up a payment plan—just like regular families do with these kinds of things."

"You do love me," Emma whispered. She almost couldn't believe it. She knew Joshua didn't trust easily; he'd said as much when he talked about his childhood. He knew what her family was like; he'd seen the worst of her stepfather. He would understand it wouldn't be easy for her to love someone again, either.

Joshua grinned and nodded. "You, Tommy and little 'Night-night'. I love all of you with my whole heart."

Joshua bent down and kissed her, really kissed her this time.

"Just like regular families," Emma repeated his words. What a wonderful thing. "I love you, too, Joshua Spencer, and I don't need any more time to say I'll marry you."

"You will?" Joshua said, his face beaming.

She nodded, and he leaned over and kissed her again.

"Oh, and I'm fixing up the Durham house so you can stay there when you come home with the baby," Joshua said in a rush. "Any colors you want, furniture, whatever, just let me know."

"You have a house for us?" Emma asked in delight.

"A room for Tommy," Joshua said. "His is yellow. And a nursery painted white with bright red and blue pillows on the rocker. A guest room for Max if he wants to come and stay a while. And then a master bedroom for—"

"For us?" Emma finished the sentence for him. "Painted in lilac, I'm guessing."

"I wanted you to like it," Joshua said.

Emma smiled. "Oh, I like it. All of it."

Then Emma leaned up on one elbow and pulled Joshua's head back down with her other hand. This time she kissed him, long and hard. When she finished, she murmured, "We'll be home together soon."

Epilogue

Three months later

Emma, in her shell-pink wedding dress, and Bailey, in her traditional ivory gown, stood side by side and looked down the grassy lane to the lilac-covered arch where Mark and Joshua stood in their black tuxedos. It was late morning on an early summer day, and the sun was shining. Doris June was walking to the electric keyboard powered by the generator hidden behind the lilac bushes. Soon she would start playing the wedding march.

"It's perfect," Bailey murmured as she looked over at Emma.

Emma nodded. She and Bailey, with input from their grooms, had planned this day together. Emma had never had a moment that felt so right. She knew she belonged here. Last month she'd had her baby tested to prove that little Aaron Eli Rosen was Junior's son. It hadn't been the money that convinced her to do so. She had finally realized that this would mean Aaron would have Rosie for a big sister. She couldn't deprive her baby of that. She and Joshua both felt that this place, with these people, was their legacy.

Even now, Rosie and Tommy were impatiently waiting off to the side. They were charged with pushing the two-seater buggy, loaded down with the two babies, along the white carpet ahead of the brides. Tommy didn't know it yet, but fifteen minutes earlier Gabe had told Emma that the judge had reviewed the items their stepfather had sent after Gabe located him, and the judge had given custody of Tommy to her and Joshua. For now, though, Tommy was focused on the wedding. Both Rosie and Tommy were going to scatter an abundance of flower petals along the path, and they each held a little bag with the respective wedding rings.

Finally, the sounds of the wedding march poured out of the keyboard, and Bailey and Emma glanced at each other.

"Now," they said in unison and took their first step down the white-carpet aisle. They were both holding lilac bouquets, and the smell followed them as they walked toward the arch. Finally, the fragrance covered the rows of white straight-backed chairs and all of their guests. Everyone was there, even Cupid who sat in his decorated cage beside Max at the end of one of the guest rows. Max planned to go back to the mountain after the wedding, but he'd accepted their invitation to come back in April to spend a week with them for Easter.

Emma stood facing Joshua, and Bailey faced Mark when the minister started their ceremony with prayer. Heartfelt assurances of love and commitment were spoken, and then finally it was time to say the vows.

Emma spoke her commitment in unison with Bailey, but she hardly noticed the other woman. She spoke her love directly to Joshua as he had just spoken his vows to her.

All too quickly, the vows were over and the minister was saying, "You may now kiss your brides."

A squawk sounded loud at that point, and Cupid screeched from his bedecked cage, "Kiss the brides! Kiss the brides!"

Everyone laughed and applauded. Emma leaned into Joshua. "Did you know about this?"

He smiled. "The kids and Max have been training that bird for weeks."

Another squawk went up. "Kiss the brides! Kiss the brides!"

"I think we're going to have lots of reminders," Joshua said with a grin.

Emma lifted her face for the kiss. She had no quarrel with that bird.

* * * * *

If you liked this story,
pick up these other heartwarming books
from Janet Tronstad:

Easter in Dry Creek
Dry Creek Daddy
His Dry Creek Inheritance

Available now from Love Inspired!

Find more great reads at www.LoveInspired.com

Dear Reader,

Many of you have written asking for more Dry Creek stories, and I am pleased to add to the number with this book. It is a follow-up to *His Dry Creek Inheritance*, which was released in February 2021. This story is separate but connected, and you'll want to read them both.

This book is special to me because it talks about trusting others. We live in a broken world, and it is not always easy to know who to trust and how to trust. I am hoping this story will encourage you in discovering that in your life.

As always, I would like to connect with you. You can find me on Facebook under Janet Tronstad. I love chitchatting there so leave a comment when you stop by. You can also email me from my website at www.janettronstad.com. I hope to see you soon in either place.

Sincerely yours,

Janet Tronstad

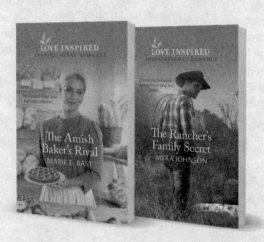

Get 4 **FREE REWARDS!**

We'll send you 2 FREE Books plus 2 FREE Mystery Gifts.

Love Inspired books feature uplifting stories where faith helps guide you through life's challenges and discover the promise of a new beginning.

FREE Value Over $20

YES! Please send me 2 FREE Love Inspired Romance novels and my 2 FREE mystery gifts (gifts are worth about $10 retail). After receiving them, if I don't wish to receive any more books, I can return the shipping statement marked "cancel." If I don't cancel, I will receive 6 brand-new novels every month and be billed just $5.24 each for the regular-print edition or $5.99 each for the larger-print edition in the U.S., or $5.74 each for the regular-print edition or $6.24 each for the larger-print edition in Canada. That's a savings of at least 13% off the cover price. It's quite a bargain! Shipping and handling is just 50¢ per book in the U.S. and $1.25 per book in Canada.* I understand that accepting the 2 free books and gifts places me under no obligation to buy anything. I can always return a shipment and cancel at any time. The free books and gifts are mine to keep no matter what I decide.

Choose one: ☐ **Love Inspired Romance**
Regular-Print
(105/305 IDN GNWC)

☐ **Love Inspired Romance**
Larger-Print
(122/322 IDN GNWC)

Name (please print)

Address   Apt. #

City   State/Province   Zip/Postal Code

Email: Please check this box ☐ if you would like to receive newsletters and promotional emails from Harlequin Enterprises ULC and its affiliates. You can unsubscribe anytime.

> Mail to the **Harlequin Reader Service:**
> **IN U.S.A.:** P.O. Box 1341, Buffalo, NY 14240-8531
> **IN CANADA:** P.O. Box 603, Fort Erie, Ontario L2A 5X3

Want to try 2 free books from another series! Call 1-800-873-8635 or visit www.ReaderService.com.

*Terms and prices subject to change without notice. Prices do not include sales taxes, which will be charged (if applicable) based on your state or country of residence. Canadian residents will be charged applicable taxes. Offer not valid in Quebec. This offer is limited to one order per household. Books received may not be as shown. Not valid for current subscribers to Love Inspired Romance books. All orders subject to approval. Credit or debit balances in a customer's account(s) may be offset by any other outstanding balance owed by or to the customer. Please allow 4 to 6 weeks for delivery. Offer available while quantities last.

Your Privacy—Your information is being collected by Harlequin Enterprises ULC, operating as Harlequin Reader Service. For a complete summary of the information we collect, how we use this information and to whom it is disclosed, please visit our privacy notice located at corporate.harlequin.com/privacy-notice. From time to time we may also exchange your personal information with reputable third parties. If you wish to opt out of this sharing of your personal information, please visit readerservice.com/consumerschoice or call 1-800-873-8635. **Notice to California Residents**—Under California law, you have specific rights to control and access your data. For more information on these rights and how to exercise them, visit corporate.harlequin.com/california-privacy.   LIR21R

"Oscar will be perfect for your needs," Ruby assured Aaron, reaching down to scratch the poodle's head.

"That froufrou dog? No way, ma'am. Not gonna happen."

"Excuse me?" She'd expected him to hesitate but not downright reject her idea.

"Look, Ruby, if you like Oscar so much, then keep him for yourself. I need a man's dog by my side, not some... some..."

"Poodle?" Ruby suggested, her eyebrows disappearing beneath her long ginger bangs.

"Right. Lead me to where you keep the German shepherds, and I'll pick one out myself."

"Hmm," Ruby said, rubbing her chin as if considering his request, although she really wasn't. "No."

"No?"

"No," she repeated firmly. "First off, we don't currently have a German shepherd as part of our program."

"I'd even take a pit bull." He was beginning to sound desperate.

"Look, Aaron. Either you're going to have to learn to trust me or you may as well just leave now before we start. This isn't going to work unless you're ready to listen to me and do whatever I tell you to do."

His eyebrows furrowed. "I understand chain of command, ma'am. There were many times as a marine when I didn't exactly agree with my superiors, but I understood why it was important to follow orders."

"Okay. Let's go with that."

"For me," Aaron continued, "following orders is black-and-white. My marines' lives under my command often depended on it. But as you can see, I'm having difficulty making that transition in this situation. We're not talking people's lives here."

"I disagree. We're very much talking lives—*yours*. You may not yet have a clear vision of what you'll be able to do with Oscar, but a service dog can make all the difference."

"Yes, but you just insisted the best dog for me is a *poodle*. I'm sorry, but if you knew anything about me at all, you'd know the last dog in the world I'd choose would be a poodle."

"And yet I still believe I'm right," said Ruby with a wry smile. Somehow, she had to convince this man she knew what she was doing. "I carefully studied your file before you arrived, Aaron, and specially selected Oscar for you to work with. I'm the expert here. So how are we going to get over this hurdle?"

"I have orders to make this work. How will it look if I give up before I even start the process?" He shook his head. "No. Don't answer that. It will look as if I wasn't able to complete my mission. That's never going to happen. I'll *always* pull through, no matter what."

Don't miss
The Marine's Mission *by Deb Kastner,*
available July 2021 wherever
Love Inspired books and ebooks are sold.

LoveInspired.com

LIEXP0621

IF YOU ENJOYED THIS BOOK, DON'T MISS NEW EXTENDED-LENGTH NOVELS FROM LOVE INSPIRED!

In addition to the Love Inspired books you know and love, we're excited to introduce even more uplifting stories in a longer format, with more inspiring fresh starts and page-turning thrills!

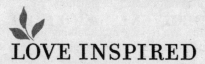

LOVE INSPIRED

Stories to uplift and inspire.

Fall in love with stories of faith, forgiveness and hope. Be inspired by characters overcoming life's challenges, and the promise of new beginnings.

LOOK FOR THESE LOVE INSPIRED TITLES ONLINE AND IN THE BOOK DEPARTMENT OF YOUR FAVORITE RETAILER!

LITRADE0621

LOVE INSPIRED
INSPIRATIONAL ROMANCE

UPLIFTING STORIES OF FAITH, FORGIVENESS AND HOPE.

Join our social communities to connect with other readers who share your love!

Sign up for the Love Inspired newsletter at **LoveInspired.com** to be the first to find out about upcoming titles, special promotions and exclusive content.

CONNECT WITH US AT:

f Facebook.com/LoveInspiredBooks

🐦 Twitter.com/LoveInspiredBks

Facebook.com/groups/HarlequinConnection

LISOCIAL2020